STRANGER THAN FICTION

◆ DEVIANT MAGIC ◆   BOOK FOUR

Scott Colby

DEVIANT MAGIC BOOK FOUR: STRANGER THAN FICTION
Copyright © 2021 Scott Colby. All rights reserved.

Published by Outland Entertainment LLC
3119 Gillham Road
Kansas City, MO 64109

Founder/Creative Director: Jeremy D. Mohler
Editor-in-Chief: Alana Joli Abbott

ISBN: 978-1-954255-14-2
EBOOK ISBN: 978-1-954255-15-9
Worldwide Rights
Created in the United States of America

Editor: Gwendolyn N. Nix
Cover Illustration: Ann Marie Cochran
Cover Design: Jeremy D. Mohler
Interior Layout: Mikael Brodu

Visit **outlandentertainment.com** to see more, or follow us on our Facebook Page **facebook.com/outlandentertainment/**

THE DEVIANT MAGIC
STORY SO FAR...

A Date with Death introduced Council of Intelligence Driff, an elven agent on the take dispatched to investigate a small town in rural Illinois where no one can die. Driff discovered that the local reaper, having spiraled down into a deep depression due to a recent breakup, had been shirking his deathly duties. When our hero's attempt to solve this problem with the aid of a group of local losers blew up in all their faces, Driff learned that the strange events in Harksburg were just part of the devious Witch's plot to temporarily dispatch an elven hero and rob him of the Ether, a powerful magic he can only lose upon dying.

That magic became important in Shotgun, when failed family man Roger Brooks discovered it in his silverware drawer and it bonded to his old ten gauge. The elves returned him to their capital, Evitankari, and declared him their Pintiri—a warrior and figurehead with a position in their legislative body, the Combined Council. Roger eventually teamed up with Driff and the reunited Brooks family to fend off the Witch and put an end to a newly restored demon warlord long thought dead. The story you're about to enjoy begins mere hours after that final battle.

Diary of a Fairy Princess doesn't have much to do with any of this (yet), but it's a fun tale of revolution in a strange magic city as told by the titular heroine in a style all her own. Notably, it implies that the Witch may not be quite as malicious as she's seemed.

Which brings me to the matter at hand: *Stranger than Fiction*. With most of Evitankari's leadership dead or scattered, Driff and Roger prepare to circle the wagons around the resources remaining to them. There's blood in the water, however, and a shapeshifting shark's zeroing in for the kill—but he's not interested in hunting alone...

Also, you know those epilogues at the end of young adult fiction that depict the heroes all grown up and happy with smiling children who are sure to turn out just as awesome as their parents? Yeah, those are bullshit.

— PROLOGUE —

*Excerpt from Chapter 47 of Lazarus Jones
and the Lightning Club: Final Showdown*

You are done for."

Headmaster Aldern—smoking, bloody, his body still spasming with the aftershocks of magical lightning—collapsed to the dirty stone floor and didn't get back up. A ragged gasp squeaked out through his chapped lips.

Kron the Withered leered down at his fallen opponent and cackled. His twisted, emaciated body quivered evilly beneath uncounted layers of tattered gray and black robes.

"Well," Lazzy said to the Lightning Club, "that's not good."

Dash leaned past his friend to peer around the corner of the tunnel leading into Kron's cavernous lair. "Yeah. This is definitely not part of the plan."

Keighlan grabbed them both by the high collars of their school uniforms and yanked them back into hiding. "We have to retreat," she said sternly. Beside her, Gearix adjusted her thick glasses and nodded in meek agreement.

Dash stuck his head back out as soon as Keighlan released her grip. "What's he taking from the headmaster?"

Kron reached into Aldern's robes and tore an amulet from the headmaster's neck. The wrinkled sorcerer stared at his prize with hungry eyes. "Thank you for delivering this to me, brother. With its power I can finally free the archdemon!"

"No way!" Dash hissed. "Kron's the headmaster's brother!"

Lazzy, peering around the corner with his friend once more, shook his head sadly. "That amulet..."

Keighlan pulled them back again. "Seriously guys, it's time to go!" Gearix repeated her previous nod.

But Lazzy wasn't listening. Resolve burning hot in his chest, he stood up straight and buttoned his jacket.

"I know that look," Dash said with a cocky smile.

"We're not going anywhere!" Lazzy declared. His bright blue eyes turned to steel. "We solved the troll's riddle. We tracked down the warlock's diary. We escaped Balacath's trap and killed the hellhound. We put all the clues together and found Kron the Withered's lair behind the blackboard of our Advanced Hex Removal classroom, defeated Balacath once and for all, and tricked Headmaster Aldern into coming here to face Kron for us. We can't run." He surveyed his friends, all of whom stared up at him in awe. "This is our responsibility. We will face Kron the Withered—and we will win!"

Gearix leapt to her feet and pumped her tiny fist. "Yeah!"

Dash stood. "Let's get 'em, Laz."

Keighlan remained seated. "How, exactly, are we going to do that?"

Lazzy smiled. "With a power Kron has never possessed and will never understand." He offered Keighlan his hand. "Help me, K."

She frowned. "I don't know about this..."

"Enough!" Kron's terrible voice boomed through the tight space. "Come out here and let me get a look at you."

The Lightning Club froze. Gearix's lower lip began to quiver. Dash peed a little.

Lazzy was the first to regain his composure. "Come on. If he wants us, he's got us."

One by one they rounded the corner and stepped into Kron's cavernous lair. Lazzy, the handsome young hero with the heart of gold. Gearix, freckled and lanky and nervous. Dash, Lazzy's cocksure best friend. And Keighlan, the beauty and the brains of the Lightning Club's whole operation. This was it: their moment, their big showdown, the confrontation they'd been working toward since they first deciphered the weird runes that kept appearing on their homeroom's blackboard.

They weren't ready. Three of them knew it. The fourth, well...

"You're not getting away with this, Kron!" Lazzy shouted.

The twisted old man cackled. He clutched the amulet in his bony fingers like it was the only thing in the world that mattered. At his feet, Aldern gasped for breath. "Kids. Run."

Lazzy snatched Keighlan's hand in his own and took a defiant step forward. "No. We're not leaving. Kron, return the medallion and turn yourself in!"

"Or what?" Kron asked, his voice tinged with genuine curiosity.

"Or you're the one who's done for!"

The ancient sorcerer rolled his rheumy eyes. "And how exactly are you going to make that come to pass?"

Lazzy tried to take another step toward Kron but Keighlan held him back. "I did a service for the fairy queen," Lazzy replied, undeterred, "and in return she granted me this blessing: as long as she who loves me most is by my side, evil shall do me no harm!"

Kron's malicious yellow smile made them all flinch. "Is that so?"

"Yes!" Lazzy shouted. "Keighlan and I love each other! You have no power over us, you evil bastard!"

Kron laughed again. "Looks to me like the girl might have a little something to say about that."

Beside Lazzy, Keighlan was shaking. The others had never seen her look so small and vulnerable. It sunk their spirits. She closed her eyes and bowed her head.

"K," Lazzy said softly, "what's wrong?"

Keighlan's face flushed and tears streamed down her cheeks. "Damn it, Lazarus!" she snapped. "I don't love you!"

Those four simple words, stated so bluntly and so angrily, tore a ragged hole deep in Lazzy's chest. "That's nonsense!" He blinked at her in disbelief. "What about that night we shared my sleeping bag in the Foreboding Woods?"

"Gnomes stole my pack and it was cold out."

"Or when we got drunk on azacea at the fairy queen's reception and I carried you back to your room?"

She shrugged. "Thanks?"

"Or when I broke Balacath's spell over you at the spring formal, and we slow danced until the chaperones made us go home?"

She cringed away from him. "I'm sorry. I was so relieved to be free of Balacath, and I knew Dash would never ask me to dance, so..."

Lazzy let his grip on Keighlan's hand go slack. For a moment she stared down at the space where his fingers had been, then she darted over to Dash and buried her head in his chest. He hesitantly wrapped an arm around her shoulders and shot his best friend a look of utter shock.

"That's it, then," Lazarus Jones croaked. The confident boy seemed to deflate, his heart well and truly broken—and their one chance to stand up to Kron shattered along with it. Lazzy's obsession with Keighlan and his inability to interpret their friendship as just that had doomed them all. He felt like such a fool.

Pyres of purple energy burst to life in Kron the Withered's hands. "That's enough teenage angst for one day. You did well to make it this far, Lazarus Jones, but your story goes no further."

The Lightning Club steeled themselves for the end. If this was truly it, at least they'd get to go out together. Lazzy and Dash exchanged a brotherly nod, the girl who'd briefly but spectacularly come between them forgotten. Keighlan clutched Dash as tight as she could. Gearix, desperate to reach Lazzy, tripped over her own big feet. He caught her—barely—and pulled her up straight.

"Lazzy," Gearix whispered, her green eyes glistening and twice their normal size, "I love you."

Kron clapped his hands together and sent a blast of violet death spiraling toward the Lightning Club. It struck Lazzy and Gearix first...

...and bounced right back, reflected like a sunbeam off a mirror. Kron the Withered barely had time to register what was happening before his own spell enveloped him. The evil warlock vanished in a puff of smoke, leaving nothing behind but a pile of ash and Headmaster Aldern's amulet.

The sudden silence in the cavern was deafening.

"We're alive," Dash muttered. Keighlan turned her head and surveyed the scene with one open eye.

Lazzy didn't care. He pulled Gearix close and pressed his lips to hers. She didn't hesitate to shove her tongue right into his mouth. He lurched back in shock and surprise and then went with it. Gearix felt good.

"Kids?" Aldern mumbled. "A little help here?"

— CHAPTER ONE —

Goody's, the most popular dive bar in the ancient neighborhood of Evitankari known as Old Ev, was packed to bursting with elves celebrating Roger Brooks's victory against Axzar and the Witch just a few hours prior. It was a tiny, claustrophobic space to begin with, which meant any single movement in any direction resulted in a chain of additional movements spreading outward in all directions like a ripple in a pond. Conversation wasn't so much a dull roar as a collection of several dozen screaming competitions struggling mightily to outdo each other. None of those in attendance cared about the AM hour, which in polite society is typically considered far too early to get that intoxicated. Elves and polite society, it turns out, go together not so much like oil and water but more like a tomato and a sledgehammer. It's not pretty.

Also not pretty: the expression on Lazzy's face. Dash couldn't decide if Lazzy looked constipated, utterly depressed, or just disgusted. He settled on "constipressgusted," took a long swig from his giant glass stein of cheap swill, and leaned back against their booth's hard wooden bench to watch the pants-suited businesswoman doing a keg stand in the corner. Yes, Goody's allows keg stands—but only on special occasions, like the Pintiri's birthday, Secretary's Day, or, to be honest, most Wednesdays.

"It's like we're not even here," Keighlan, Dash's wife, muttered from beside him. The remains of four extra dirty martinis—strategically ordered all at once for efficiency's sake and subsequently slammed back with the same competence and economy—surrounded her like a tiny glass honor guard. She'd been tracing increasingly malformed figure eights on the skin of Dash's muscular right forearm for the last twenty minutes, a nervous habit that meant she had a problem that required her husband's undivided attention. Dash had decided to ignore her in the hopes that she'd get angry and cause a scene so they could go home already.

"My glass has been empty for ten minutes," Lazzy moaned, his babyface somehow pinching itself left and right and up and down all at the same time. Short and thin as a rail, Lazzy had always made up for his lack of stature with a powerful personality and the sort of can-do attitude that's mostly gone extinct outside of home renovation shows. "We haven't had to buy our own drinks in this town...ever," Lazzy continued.

"Had to happen eventually," Dash said, trying to keep the strain out of his voice. He was glad no one in Goody's was paying them any mind. Adoring fans and would-be hangers-on had been all up in his business for far too long. "We had a good run."

"Doesn't mean we have to like it," Gearix, Lazzy's wife, mused from her spot slumped in the corner. Strands of her wispy red hair stuck oddly in the nooks and crannies of the wall. The splash of freckles that had been a mark of shame in her youth now made Dash's heart flutter. She'd had a single small beer and called it a morning. She'd always been the quiet, introspective one of the group, content to let the other three take the lead and garner all the attention while she worked things out in the background. Dash could tell from the tightness in her lips and the set of her jaw that she was busy at work doing just that.

"We shouldn't have to like it," Lazzy declared with a slight slur. "Eighteen years ago, we—just a precocious quartet of teenagers barely into our third year in the academy—single-handedly thwarted Kron the Withered's attempt to destroy Evitankari. We're heroes! None of these people would even be here without us!"

"We had a good run," Dash repeated. Lazzy could ramble on for hours if no one derailed him, and Dash had an upcoming and urgent appointment with his recliner, his home brew, and a Spurs/Bulls game later that afternoon. "Maybe give it a few days, Laz. That human and his wife and Council of Intelligence Driff are probably just the flavor of the month."

"Or they're next year's model," Gearix said wistfully, "and we're the old junkers on the back lot, ruined by time and depreciation to the point that even the dealership's most desperate salesmen won't bring anyone out to see us."

"I get to be a Mazda Miata," Keighlan replied sleepily. "Remember when we rented one of those in Florida, D?"

This was Dash's chance. "I'm pretty sure that was some sort of Chevy, K." It absolutely wasn't and he knew it.

She blinked at him in surprise. "No, it was a yellow Miata. With leather seats."

Lazzy grabbed the shirt of the nearest patron walking past. "Hey. You know who I am?" The guy looked down at him, scowled, and slid deeper into the crowd.

Dash took another drink from his beer to steel his nerves. "It was a Chevy Camaro," he said bluntly. "Blue."

Keighlan recoiled from him in sloppy drunken horror. "It was not!"

In the corner, Gearix idly traced her finger along a ragged heart carved into the wall.

"It was definitely a Chevy," Dash said.

Lazzy leaned out of the booth and yanked a woman's skirt to get her attention. "Miss, do you know who I am?"

She spun around and slapped him in the face. "Quit it, perv!" She melted away into the masses behind a wall of angry male companions.

"D, I can't believe you! That was definitely a Miata!"

"Chevy."

"And why are you so intent on correcting me in front of our friends?"

"Because you're wrong."

A broad shadow darkened the booth. Dash looked up to find an obese, red-faced elf in an ill-fitting gray business suit had squeezed himself into the narrow space between their table and the three dudes still glowering at Lazzy.

"Do you know who I am?" Lazzy asked.

The newcomer nodded. A few drops of sweat from his broad forehead spattered the table. "I'm familiar with each of you. Lazzy, the headstrong hero with a heart of gold. Gearix, the former ugly duckling who loves Lazzy with all her heart. Keighlan, the energetic overachiever with a solution for every problem." He paused. "And Dash, the sidekick."

Too stunned for words, Dash stared up at the wide elf in dumb shock. Sure, everyone in Evitankari knew their story backward and forward, but few would ever describe his role in such dismissive terms—even if they agreed with that assessment in private.

"And you're Council of Economics Granger," Gearix said coolly. "To what do we owe the pleasure?"

"I'm here on business, of course," Granger replied with a Cheshire Cat grin. "And today's business is that human Pintiri you're all so jealous of."

"We're not jealous!" Lazzy protested. "We just don't want to be forgotten."

"Fuck that," Keighlan slurred. "I'm jealous."

Granger shrugged. "Either way, I believe I can be of assistance."

"How?" Gearix asked, clearly skeptical.

Granger's grin expanded into a double-wide, complete with attached deck. "I have reason to believe the Pintiri's 'defeat' of the demon lord Axzar didn't go exactly as the official story would have us believe."

"I knew it!" Lazzy shouted as if he'd just discovered the secret of cold fusion.

"Dirty humans," Keighlan muttered.

Dash ignored the excited glances bouncing around the table and drained the remainder of his beer as he turned Granger's words over in his mind. *Gee*, he thought angrily, *doesn't all that sound familiar.*

— CHAPTER TWO —

When can we go home?"

Roger Brooks, disheveled and dirty and sweaty and reeking of stress and exertion, stared at Samantha like she'd asked him to reveal his deepest, darkest secret on national television. Middle-aged and kind of average in build, he was handsome in a goofy sort of way. The poor guy obviously needed a shower and a nap, but he'd insisted on speaking with his daughter in private upon his return to Merrowood, the Pintiri's private residence. So there they were, sitting side by side atop a firm mattress and 800-thread count sheets in the spare bedroom Sam had claimed as her own.

His lack of an answer was a response unto itself. "Alright, then," Sam said sheepishly. "What did you want to talk about?"

He looked down at the shotgun in his lap. It was an old, worn, terrible thing, a pair of dull metal barrels attached to a cheap wooden stock. It had been his father's a long time ago, and it had spent most of Sam's life locked in a cabinet in Roger's bedroom closet. Now it housed the Ether, the most powerful magic in the elven inventory. That shotgun had gone from neglected step-child to world-famous globetrotting pop star practically overnight.

"Sam, I need your help," Roger said. Sam had never seen that sort of desperation in his eyes. He'd always been an easy-going but super dorky guy, the sort of parent you don't want chaperoning your high school dances but who you're glad is there for family movie nights and those times you just need to cry out all your adolescent angst. As far as dads go, she could've done a lot worse and probably not much better. Seeing him so haggard and cornered just felt wrong.

"You know I've got your back," she replied with a friendly punch to his solid shoulder. "None of these magic weirdos stand a chance against the two of us."

He smiled and squeezed Sam's knee. "My thoughts exactly. Most of the people I thought I could trust in this godforsaken city are either dead or proven traitors. You're the only one here I know I can rely on."

Sam hadn't expected something that melodramatic. She scrambled for a joke while collecting her thoughts. "Ricky already said no, didn't he?"

"Your brother's ten," Roger replied with a smile. "He's in charge of infiltrating the local elementary school for me. And your mother's got enough on her plate."

That's not the way Sam would've put it, but whatever. Biting back a "that's not my mother" quip required a sincere force of effort and a little bit of blood from her tongue. Talora looked like Virginia Brooks the way a cantaloupe resembles a watermelon: the shape was mostly right, but none of the details fit. Supposedly this was a side effect of the process that had awakened some long-dormant magic the family had never suspected she possessed. Sam wasn't buying it. Talora's body may have been similar to Virginia's, but her mind wasn't. Her magic was fueled by her memories, and she'd burned through every last one of them. Sam understood why Dad clung to her—their relationship had turned rocky in the end, and now (supposedly) here was a version of the woman he loved, unburdened by what had driven them apart and ripe for a fresh start.

Sam decided to move on. "Okay. So. What are my duties and title? How's the dental plan?"

"Jeez, I didn't realize I was going to have to print you business cards," Roger said with a comically slow shake of his head. "I need backup, essentially, that I can hide as my innocent-looking-yet-hawk-eyed assistant. You'll accompany me to all formal meetings and gatherings and just be another pair of eyes on everything, and you'll learn every single last tiny little thing about this place you possibly can."

"Because I'm a history major and I'm smarter than you?"

"Yes. How does Special Assistant to the Pintiri sound?"

"I'd prefer Chief of Staff. More gravitas, fewer made-up-sounding words."

"Done."

"Do I get a magic shotgun? Or maybe one of those tiny pistols elegant-but-deadly ladies used to hide up the sleeves of their prissy dresses?"

He scratched his chin. "I probably should find you some sort of protective talisman or something."

It took Sam a moment to realize he was serious. *So this*, she thought, *is the new normal.* She wasn't sure which part of her father's response was more unsettling: the reminder that magic was indeed real, or that she might genuinely need some form of protection from people or things looking to do her harm. Her biggest worry back at school was getting up in time to hit the course registration site before everyone else to avoid those dreaded eight a.m. classes. Funny how that whole "not a morning person" thing paled in comparison to "might get blown to bits by an evil sorcerer's fireball."

"Remember: no gold," Sam replied. "It makes me itch. And I'd prefer earrings over a necklace or a ring."

"I'll see what I can do. Any other questions?"

She pursed her lips and feigned further deliberation. "Salary?"

He shrugged. "I haven't had to pay for a thing since I got here. I'll make sure you're on whatever tab I've been running."

"Good enough," Sam replied merrily, offering her right hand. "Mr. Brooks, you've got yourself a Chief of Staff."

Roger took his daughter's hand and pumped it happily. "Welcome aboard, Ms. Brooks. I suspect you'll do fine things for our little enterprise. Fine things!"

An elf in a black trench coat and a pair of spectacles materialized in the center of the room. Father and daughter both jumped in surprise. Sam's heart leapt into her chest.

"Good," Council of Intelligence Driff said in his dull, precise monotone. "Let's get to work."

"What the hell?" Sam snapped. "How did you get in here?"

"I turned invisible, followed your father up the stairs and down the hall, and slipped inside before he shut the door."

Sam didn't trust magic, and seeing it in action tore her already frayed nerves. She remained self-aware enough, however, to realize that showing weakness to the elves—especially to this elf in particular—wouldn't do her father any favors. The Council of Intelligence's behavior reminded her of Robby Randall, scourge of her public school system. Robby loved keeping the other kids off guard and under his thumb by being unpredictable and aggressive. In elementary school, he became notorious for hiding art supplies, spitting in desserts, and delivering the sorts of wedgies that caused nightmares for days. He progressed into psychological warfare as a teenager, relying upon an impressive list of creative nicknames and a true talent for identifying and exploiting that one thing his victims absolutely could not stand. She'd learned long ago that the best way to deflect Robby was to throw something similarly obnoxious right back at him. Maybe something like that would work with Driff.

"As Chief of Staff, I forbid you from doing that ever again. And you're banned from the employee pancake breakfast for one month."

He cocked his head and looked down his hawkish nose at Sam like she was some sort of science experiment gone awry. She hated the way elves often tried looking through her rather than at her, like they couldn't believe she was there and speaking to them and they wanted to make sure she wasn't just another figment of their excessively active imaginations. Sam tilted her own head, frowned, and stared right back at the Council of Intelligence.

Roger poked her in the side. "Remember my earlier comment about not being able to trust anyone around here? Driff's walking, talking proof of that."

"Oooh, what did he do?" Sam asked scandalously. "Did he look at your screen during a local two-player game? Eat the last donut in the Pintiri's office kitchenette? Wait...he reheated fish in the lunchroom microwave, didn't he? What a jerk!"

Driff's eyes narrowed and his head shifted even further to the side.

"Nothing quite that bad," Roger replied. "He strung me along as a friend and confidant, but he'd been working for the Witch all along. The one that kidnapped you and Ricky, remember? Anyway, he double-crossed her in the end and the entire city now thinks he's a fucking hero. He's damn lucky he had an audience at the end there, too, or he'd be rotting in the same hole I threw the Witch's brother."

Sam had never heard her father speak that way. He'd spent the last twenty-something years mopping floors and cleaning toilets as a high school janitor, a profession that didn't exactly lend itself to threatening speeches or proclamations of ultimate authority. It didn't really fit him, and Sam could tell by the tremors in his hands that he knew it—and that, she realized, was why he really needed her to be his Chief of Staff.

Driff rolled his eyes and sighed. "Endlessly recounting the past will just waste time better spent preparing for the future."

"And I assume from your cold confidence and general OCD demeanor that you've already got some idea how to do that," Sam said.

He straightened and pushed his spectacles up on his nose. "Of course. Including you in our work is merely step one."

She glared at her father. "Wait a minute. This whole assistant thing was his idea?"

Roger nodded.

"You don't think this is some sort of setup?"

"Even if it is, it's a good idea. Driff's a selfish asshole, but he's no dope."

"Thanks," the elf said.

"Just shoot him now," Sam suggested. "I won't tell."

"I'd kind of love to, but that's the wrong move. Here's the point, Sam: I understand what makes this guy tick, he's been useful to me in the past, and he knows more about what's going on than anyone. He's on Team Brooks until the next time he fucks up."

"Telling me exactly how much you distrust me may not be your smartest play, even if you're working on some complex reverse-psychology idea," Driff muttered.

"Agreed," Sam chirped. "You should've cleared this with your Chief of Staff first. Please vet all future moves in 'the game' through my office before making them."

Roger sighed and glanced at Driff. "She gets that attitude from her mother."

"Clearly."

"Personality assessments of senior staff members can wait," Sam said. "What's this grand plan of yours, Drifford?"

"It's just Driff." He pushed his spectacles up on his nose again. "We're at a unique point in elven history. Our ranks of sorcerers are at an historic low due to a recent terrorist attack."

"His fault," Roger whispered.

"The Combined Council, a governing body of eight individuals, has been reduced to a group of two: Roger Brooks and myself. The Councils of War, Agriculture, Sorcery, Medicine, and Economics stand vacant. The man who currently holds the Mongan position that serves as the Pintiri's second and heir to the Ether—the Witch's brother—is 'rotting in a hole' and will need to be replaced."

"Also his fault."

"The location of former Council of War Pike, known for his angry, violent outbursts, is currently unknown. He may be harboring a dangerous grudge."

"Definitely his fault."

"The Witch is still out there somewhere and planning her next move against us. The leadership of the demonic Tallisker corporation, with whom Evitankari conducts several important lines of business, has been decimated, rendering the immediate future of the company unpredictable at best. The Shala'ni, exiled from Evitankari, are continuing their assault on Tallisker's major regional offices. Talvayne, the fairy capital, has ceased all contact. Dissident groups within elven culture may view the current situation as the perfect time to make a grab for increased power and influence. And the mysterious shape-shifters who aided us against the Witch could be anywhere and up to anything."

"Any of that his fault?" Sam whispered.

"Nah," Roger said dismissively. "I gather all those things were pains in the ass long before he got involved."

Driff continued without acknowledging the interruption. "Evitankari has been severely weakened and her allies and enemies knocked into disarray. This suggests that malicious action toward the elven nation is extremely likely in the near term. Although several options and contingencies exist for securing our current assets and rebuilding our strength, these things will take time. We are severely vulnerable to both external and internal attack."

"See why I need him?" Roger asked.

"Lovely," Sam snarled. "Say, did this Chief of Staff job come with any sort of non-compete clause? Just curious. You know, in case this proves to be a little too much for me."

"You're going to really hate this next part," her father mumbled.

"Our best means of thwarting the suspected attack on the elven nation is to direct that attack into an arena which we control. If we know what's coming and when, we can rally what resources remain to us to stop it."

A sinking feeling twisted a knot into Sam's stomach. "I'm going to be the bait, aren't I?"

— CHAPTER THREE —

The first order of business for the Pintiri's new Chief of Staff: the state funeral for the elves who lost their lives in the confrontation prior to Axzar's release and during the Devourer's short-lived rampage across the city.

Roger, Driff, and Sam were up until two in the morning preparing for the nine o'clock funeral and generally getting up to speed on Evitankari's current situation. They turned Merrowood's living room into a makeshift command center, although the previous Pintiri's collection of leather upholstery and shag carpet didn't lend itself well to even a semi-official meeting space. Roger, as Pintiri and man of the house, claimed an entire recliner all for himself, leaving his Chief of Staff and the Council of Intelligence together on the couch.

As the new senior member of the Combined Council, Driff's role in the funeral was to say a few words about each of the deceased, a task he was quite obviously none too thrilled about. Although his pen never stopped moving, Driff spent most of the hour it took him to crank out his first draft sighing, rolling his eyes, shaking his head, and otherwise physically implying that he disdained the task and every single one of the deceased.

Sam found it all rather distracting. "I can't tell if you're writing eulogies for dearly departed contemporaries or rage tweeting at your most hated enemies," she said, leering at him over a thick book on recent elven politics.

Driff's pen kept moving as he glanced curiously at Sam's reading material. "Let me save you the trouble and summarize: we're a bunch of assholes."

"I don't need five hundred pages to tell me that," she replied.

"Children," Roger said. The latest status reports from Evitankari's various constituencies covered his lap and the arms of the recliner like an afghan from accountant hell. "Finish your homework or no dessert."

They returned to their respective tasks. Driff toned down his annoyed mannerisms and Sam resumed her reading. The dry, flavorless text reminded her of her schoolwork—and made her wonder if she'd ever get a chance to return to it. Determined to prove herself a more mature adult than the elf on the opposite end of the couch, she banished the thought from her mind and focused on the task at hand.

"Done," Driff finally declared an hour later, stashing his pen behind his pointy ear and shoving the little pad of eulogies in Samantha's face.

"Not yet," Sam snapped as she snatched the pad away. She cleared her throat and read his precise cursive out loud. "Barten. Renowned business strategist and beloved father. History of late library books." She cocked an eyebrow and continued. "Feliciana. Top pyromancer in her class. Fondness for gin led to regular blackouts."

"Driff?" Roger asked from the recliner. "You know that's not very nice, right?"

Sam read on, skipping ahead to what she'd decided were the fun parts. "Penchant for overstaying his welcome. Not-so-secret desire to participate in vegetable-based sodomy. Stared intently at the feet of older women."

Driff pushed his spectacles up on his nose. "Traditional elven eulogies are reminiscences of personal experiences with the deceased. I am the Council of Intelligence. I know these people primarily through my department's dossiers."

"Excessive gambler. Cheated at board games. Replied to spam emails from nonexistent Nigerian princes."

"Wait," Roger said, shaking his head in confusion. "Why do you keep records of this crap?"

"Wet the bed two to five times a month. Rifled through the neighbors' trash for half-eaten desserts. Believed in aliens, sasquatch, and the long-term viability of unregulated capitalism."

"You never know when you might need to exert a bit of leverage," Driff replied, as if that explained it all.

"Twice paid for sexual relations with a troll in a bowler hat. Picked his nose and flicked it off the back porch; 10 meters personal best. Never learned the words to 'Happy Birthday.'"

"So you memorized the foibles and flaws of everyone in Evitankari?" Roger asked.

"Wouldn't you?" Driff deadpanned.

"I'll just cross off the last sentence in every entry," Samantha declared.

"Sometimes it's two sentences," Driff said. "And I reversed the format about halfway through to keep myself entertained."

"I hate you."

"Then our working relationship is off to a perfect start."

"Council of Intelligence Driff," she snarled. "Photographic memory. Giant douchebag."

Roger cackled from his recliner.

When she finally went to bed, Sam dreamed of stapling Driff's feet to the pavement in the middle of a busy street and leaving him there to get hit by a speeding bus. He exploded in a mushroom cloud of feminine hygiene products. Usually Sam was excellent at forgiving and forgetting, but apparently her subconscious was better at carrying a grudge.

She could've used another hour or two of sleep and a few more visions of Driff's terrible demise, but morning—and Merrowood's steward—were not to be delayed. The heavy velvet curtains on the room's two windows snapped open so the rising sun could punch her square in the face. "Up and at 'em!" the pixie squeaked in her tiny, feminine voice as she flittered into the room. Walinda. Dedicated servant without whom Merrowood might simply collapse. Loud, tactless, and impatient to a fault—although in certain situations that list of negatives became a huge positive.

Samantha rolled onto her back, opened her eyes, and sat up. She'd never been one of those people who felt the need to dramatize the process of getting out of bed. She wasn't a groaner, a roller, or a violent assaulter of the alarm clock. Waking up sucked, and she'd always found it best just to get it over with. "Thanks, Walinda," she muttered anxiously. The tiny woman and her telekinetic powers made her nervous.

"You're welcome, Chief," Walinda chirped. Enveloped by the soft red aura that glowed around her when she was in flight, the pixie flitted into the room to hover in front of Sam's face, flashing her trademark sassy half-grin. Her black maid's uniform was crisply pressed as usual. She was in Evitankari as part of a cultural exchange program with her home city, Talvayne, and she'd been loaned to the new Pintiri when Merrowood's previous steward quit in a burst of racist bullshit. "Breakfast is ready when you are. Your brother and your mother are already showered and dressed, so take your time. Today's outfit will be laid out here after you've freshened up."

Walinda zipped back out into the hallway before Sam could thank her again. The feeling of relief Sam felt at the pixie's departure was replaced by embarrassing guilt. Being nervous around Walinda was uncalled for; the steward was just there to help, and she performed her duties cheerfully and efficiently.

The bathroom across the hall was the nicest bathroom Sam had ever used. The word "cavernous" came to mind as she shucked her pajamas. Three or four people could've fit in the shower while another eleven or twelve waited for a turn just outside. Given the previous Pintiri's reputation, perhaps that wasn't so far-fetched.

There were no controls in that shower. According to her father, all the showers in Merrowood would start automatically when occupied and then adjust the water temperature and dispense soap and shampoo by reading the user's thoughts. When Sam stepped inside, nothing happened. She tried waving her hand underneath the shower head and the soap dispensers, but that didn't work either. Confused, she took a step back to examine things again. There definitely weren't any valves or controls anywhere in the slick white tile. It was like the thing knew she didn't particularly want a magic shower.

She leaned her head back and sighed, because of course it knew. Easily offended psychic bathroom fixtures weren't a thing Sam's previous life had prepared her to deal with and she really didn't like the idea of them poking around in her thoughts. Did the shower have access to everything happening in her mind? Was it recording or transmitting? If it could read her thoughts, could it also insert new ideas or change her perceptions? What if it misinterpreted a thought and unleashed a torrent of scalding water? Her lack of understanding contributed pretty deeply to her distrust of sorcery, she knew, but relying on such forces in mundane situations that didn't seem to require the mystical arts also felt pretty reckless.

"Get it together, girl," she muttered under her breath. "No one's going to respect a Chief of Staff who smells like dirty socks." Long, hot showers were also one of her favorite things, and she knew a good one right then and there would seriously soothe her nerves.

Samantha focused on a section of grout in between a quartet of tiles and cleared her mind. It was just a shower. There was nothing weird about it. It was a perfectly normal part of a perfectly normal bathroom. There was no reason to worry. It wasn't planting subconscious suggestions in her brain or beaming her deepest, darkest desires to Council of Intelligence Driff. It would be the best, warmest shower ever, and it would make her feel so much better about herself.

A thin stream of water trickled down onto her forehead. She yelped in response. The shower gave up. So did Samantha.

Luckily the sink worked simply by sticking something underneath the faucet. A lever mounted atop the spigot controlled the temperature—making the magic shower seem even sillier. She washed herself as best she could with a face cloth, brushed her teeth using the brush with her name taped to it, and scampered back to her room with a towel wrapped around her torso and her dirty clothes clutched tightly to her chest. Just as the pixie had promised, Sam's outfit for the day—a plain black dress with dark stockings and a reasonably comfortable pair of black pumps—was waiting for her on the bed. It all looked a few sizes too large, but each garment shrunk and shifted until it fit perfectly. She lacked the words to describe just how icky that felt.

Sam grabbed a hair tie from the small pile on the nightstand and pulled her hair back into a ponytail as she headed downstairs. Her heart pounded in her chest; breakfast with her father, her younger brother, and Talora—the woman who was supposedly her mother but who Samantha knew totally wasn't—didn't sound like a great way to start the day, mostly because she had no idea what to expect. She hated not knowing what to expect. It was a side effect of being reasonably smart and thus generally knowing how things were going to shake out.

Weird, uncomfortable situation after weird, uncomfortable situation paraded through her mind as she descended the wide marble stairs to the foyer. Talora attempting to forge some awkward mother/daughter bond over French toast. Talora offering her help with homework or boys. Talora looking at Roger with any sort of emotion. Those magically shrinking clothes weren't the only things that made her feel gross. She hoped that breakfast would turn out to be the only time in her life when heading for a funeral early seemed like a good idea.

The rest of the Brooks clan were already well into breakfast when Sam arrived in the dining room. The affair turned out more like a blind date than a family meal.

"So...Samantha," Talora said tentatively over what had to have been her fourth or fifth cup of coffee. Walinda had set her up with an outfit almost identical to what she'd left for Sam, although the shoulders of her black dress were puffier. The woman was wired; her leg jittered up and down uncontrollably. "Can I call you Sam?"

Samantha glanced anxiously at her father and then at Ricky. They were too busy stuffing their faces with pancakes, bacon, and sausage to serve as suitable distractions. "I guess," she muttered. Walinda was, supposedly, still working on Sam's plate in the kitchen, a delay she suspected wasn't entirely a coincidence.

"You're twenty?" Talora asked. Her hands shook as she lifted her mug. Sam couldn't tell if it was due to the caffeine or her own nervousness. She'd never seen her real mother's hands shake like that.

The thought inspired her to take a closer look. Talora was the right height and weight and her hair was the proper shade of blond, but her face was all wrong. Her chin was too long, her cheekbones were too high, and her eyes were too squinty. Her bearing wasn't right, her posture was too slouched, and the real Virginia Brooks never, ever would've put both of her elbows on the table. And then there were the antlers sprouting from her head—supposedly a side effect of whatever process had twisted her features and given her the ability to generate magic fire in her hands. Sam wasn't buying it; the idea that her mother would've gone along with such a thing was unfathomable. Virginia Brooks loved her family too much to consent to having her memories of them wiped out.

"Eighteen, actually," she replied. "And six months and twenty days."

Talora seemed to be briefly trying to do the math in her head to determine Samantha's birthday, then gave up. "And you're—you were—studying English?"

"History."

She squinted as if working hard to commit that tidbit to memory. Sam had never seen her real mother do that, either. "You like it?" Talora asked.

"Yeah."

"What's your favorite part?"

"My favorite part of history? Or my favorite part of studying it?"

She hesitated, considering. "Both."

"The violent executions." Sam paused. "In both cases."

"Sam," Roger growled in that special tone known to all fathers who have to pretend to be annoyed when they're actually amused. His daughter knew that tone well.

"Alright," Sam replied in the semi-huffy manner of children who understand what's going on and why but don't like it. "My favorite part of history is the Renaissance. My favorite part of studying history is how it improves my understanding of our current situation."

Talora smiled. "I bet that understanding needs some adjustment now, with all...this." Her free hand fluttered to indicate their immediate surroundings. Sam's real mother never did that, either. Virginia Brooks was not a flutterer.

But Talora's statement about history was interesting. Sam hadn't considered that. Although she understood the basic idea of Evitankari maintaining the world order and keeping magic hidden with their memory-altering narii dust, she realized she had no clue exactly how the elves had directed the course of history. Had they influenced wars and elections? Had seemingly random events actually been all a part of their plan for the planet? Her professors all would've murdered each other for the chance to find out. History—human history, at least—likely needed some serious rewriting. The prospect of learning about it was beyond exciting.

"It's just another layer," Sam said.

Walinda zipped into the room and telekinetically placed a plate of breakfast on the table in front of Samantha. The pixie hovered for a second, then she magically lifted a pancake from the plate and returned to the kitchen with it. "It's just another layer!" she called back.

Ricky snickered. Sam gave him the older sister death glare.

"I'll let you eat," Talora said politely as she backed her chair away from the table, "but I'd like to talk more soon." She snatched up her cup of coffee and fled the room. Sam knew she probably should've felt bad, but she didn't.

Roger watched Talora go, clearly waiting until she was out of earshot to say what he had to say. "Sam, that's your mother."

"No, it's not." Half of her bacon darted back into the kitchen.

"Yes, it is. She's just got a lot of catching up to do."

"Because her magic burned away all her memories? Right. Sure."

Roger laughed at her. Heartily. It stung. "You'll learn," he said, smiling like he knew some secret that made the whole situation hilarious. "Oh man, you'll learn."

Sam didn't know what that meant, so she busied herself with what was left of her breakfast. Walinda really was a heck of a cook. The pancakes were light and fluffy and delicious and the accompanying meat products were perfectly crispy but not even close to burned. There was no doubt in Sam's mind that life in Evitankari would never stop being weird and frustrating, but at least the accommodations were solid.

"Dad," Ricky said tentatively, "what's 'defenestrate?'"

Roger pushed around a few sausage links with his fork, pretending to be deep in thought. "Sounds complicated. Sam?"

"It's when you throw someone out a window."

Roger blanched. "Ricky, where'd you learn that word?"

He shrugged. "I don't know."

Father and daughter traded a look. Ricky must've picked the word up from Walinda or one of the Pintiri's Gadukah guards—most likely that Ivree weirdo, Sam decided. Ricky had always had big ears and a habit of listening in on adult conversations. Sam shook her head, dismissing it, and returned her attention to her plate. She really wished Walinda hadn't taken so much of it away.

Fifteen minutes of awkward silence later, they departed for the funeral. Talora joined them in the foyer and two of the Gadukah met them on Merrowood's front porch.

"Good morning, Pintiri," the older commando said. Commander Rynes. Grizzled, veteran leader of the Gadukah. Hasn't success-fully completed a Sunday crossword in three years, despite weekly attempts. Sam liked his gruff, no-nonsense approach immediately. "Hirace and I will escort you and your family to Willowglen."

"Thanks," Roger replied, slightly embarrassed. Sam couldn't imagine how weird it must've been to suddenly have a squad of deadly commandos at your beck and call, especially when you've been a school janitor your entire life. She bet her father wished he'd had a few of the Gadukah around for puke duty.

"Our pleasure, sir," the other commando added. Hirace. Reliable, hardworking overachiever who served as the Gadukah's medic and primary sniper. Forever trapped in and fighting to break out of the shadow of his famous uncle, former Council of War Pike. Sam cringed and tried to hide behind her father when she saw him. Her initial reaction to all this elves-and-magic stuff was somewhat less than dignified, and she'd aimed a good portion of that frustration at Hirace. She'd known their paths would cross again sooner rather than later, but she wasn't quite ready to deal with that particular embarrassment yet.

They set off. Rynes led the way and Hirace covered them from behind. Sam was less than thrilled that Talora and Ricky were coming along. She understood why the Pintiri's entire family and supposed family were expected to attend, but her brother was too young and her "mother" was too...not with it. Sam didn't want to have to babysit either one of them and she wished they could've been left behind in Merrowood. Her father had just saved the city and probably the entire world from an ancient evil too terrible for words. Surely Evitankari could've forgiven a minor funeral faux pas.

The walk to Willowglen was Sam's first look at the elven city, but she didn't get to see much. Their route took them along a series of lonely back roads slicing through the dense forests surrounding Merrowood. Dirt and stone paths branched off from the cobblestone street here and there, likely leading to other homes hidden deep in the forest. The few elves they passed acknowledged them with waves or a nod but otherwise left them alone.

They'd been walking for about ten minutes—half the distance to Willowglen—when Hirace stepped forward beside Samantha. "You're in better spirits today," he said.

Her face flushed. "Sorry about that," she said. "Not my proudest moment."

"I've heard worse," he replied. Hirace's smile reminded Sam of a cartoon frog in a children's book her mother used to read her. "I get it," he added. "We're different and the things we can do are like nothing you've ever seen."

Sam was pretty sure he didn't mean to sound like an arrogant tool. "Yeah," she said, "it's a lot to digest."

Hirace nodded. "I'm still not sure I understand it all, and I've lived it for the last twenty-five years."

She didn't buy that for a second, but she knew this wasn't the time or the place to call one of her father's allies out for being patronizing. She let the comment pass without responding.

"Anyway...I'm bothering you for a reason. The Gadukah oath binds us only to the Pintiri, but historically we've also been there for the Pintiri's family as well. If you ever need anything, just ask one of us and we'll take care of it."

"Thank you, Hirace. I'll keep that in mind." She made a mental note to ask the big goof for a box of tampons in a day or two just to watch him squirm.

Hirace wouldn't drop it. "Seriously, Sam. The Gadukah's here for you."

"You can call me Samantha," she said, probably a little more harshly than she intended. "And I got it." Ahead of them, Roger shook his head. "But thank you," she added, "for everything you've done for my father and for your service to my family."

The elf looked down at Sam as if he expected more, but she couldn't figure out what he wanted. Her approach to Driff wouldn't work here. Hirace wasn't another pointy-eared Robby Randall clone; he was the elven Walt Gentry, relentlessly helpful teacher's pet. Redirecting his energy and waiting it out would be her best strategy. "What do you know about Willowglen?" she finally asked a few paces later. She already knew everything she needed to know about the place because she'd read up on it the night before, but asking Hirace about their destination seemed like a safe way to make the guy feel useful—and to distract herself from how close Talora and her father were getting.

He perked back up. "It's really pretty. I think you'll like it." He hesitated. "But it's also where we lay our dead to rest. Fallen elves are lowered into the waters of the Origina so that the Evertree—the big willow on the island in the middle of the pond—can access their memories when we need them."

"That's...kind of creepy."

"How so?"

"Well, how do you feel about the idea of some tree rooting around inside your head when you're gone?"

If he got Sam's magnificent pun, he wasn't amused by it. "I suspect I'll be too dead to care."

"You could care now, while you're alive."

"You don't think it's wasteful to just bury the dead?"

"No. And sometimes we burn them."

"Like...for warmth?"

Sam laughed so hard she almost tripped. Ricky, who'd been watching their exchange intently, caught his sister's arm. She'd forgotten he was there. He'd always been easy to lose track of. He had an innate ability to sort of melt into the scenery and listen in to private conversation without getting caught. He was worse than Driff.

"Did I say something stupid?" Hirace asked.

Sam left it alone. "Some people prefer to have their ashes scattered in a meaningful place when they pass."

Hirace frowned. "That's kind of gross."

This time she couldn't resist. "You've seen how easily ashes get blown away by the wind, right? You could be covered in the remains of dead humans right now and you wouldn't even know it!"

"Sam," Roger said.

But the elf, to his credit, didn't even flinch. "Guess I'll just have to shower more often," he said with a smile.

Willowglen's big iron gate loomed before them at the end of the cobblestone road. Sam took a deep, worried breath. This would be the Brooks family's first formal public appearance in Evitankari and her first time in the spotlight as her father's Chief of Staff. The weight of that realization refocused her on the task at hand. Her only responsibilities during the funeral itself were to be there, keep an eye on things, and "don't do anything weird, Sam," but she still had to be front and center as an official presence. Could she even pull off official presence? She wasn't sure, and her long history of bawling her eyes out at previous funerals made her doubt she'd be able to pull it off at this one.

The park on the other side of the gate was amazing. It was home to the greenest grass and the most perfectly trimmed trees she'd ever seen. The Origina—the pond in the middle—was impossibly blue and beautiful. A giant willow lorded over it all from a tiny island in the center of that pond. Sam had read that Willowglen was the heart of Evitankari, a physical representation of the peace and serenity the elves strive so desperately to instill in a chaotic world. She'd considered that a bit heavy handed at the time, but in reality even that overcooked description didn't quite do the place justice.

As seemed to be the case with everything else in Evitankari, however, Willowglen was also the site of a really big, really strange problem: the funeral they were scheduled to attend had already started.

— CHAPTER FOUR —

"Kerval," Council of Economics Granger said solemnly as the deceased's coffin was lowered into the Origina by a foursome of beefy pallbearers. "She worked in Port, assessing incoming flammable materials for safety. Hadn't missed a day in seven years."

Dash—correction, Council of Agriculture Dash—could not have cared less. If it had been up to him, he would've still been in bed, or maybe drinking a coffee and perusing the sports news on his back porch. He certainly wouldn't have been standing hand-in-hand with Keighlan in front of a huge crowd in Willowglen while the first step in their little conspiracy played itself out. Granger's plan was more brazen than Dash was comfortable with, but the other three were all in. They'd always loved the spotlight. Keighlan, Gearix, and Lazzy all stood straight and proud in their black uniforms, almost daring someone in the crowd to say something, anything, about their unexplained ascension to the Combined Council. The citizens in attendance—thousands strong and growing as more elves streamed into the park—mostly just stared at the quartet in confusion or studied their own feet in disinterest. Dash knew exactly which contingent he'd belong to were their roles reversed.

Council of Intelligence Driff stood alone off to the side. He'd taken their arrival and Granger's motion to start the funeral early in stoic stride. Dash could almost hear the wheels turning in the elf's cold, calculating mind. The human Pintiri would likely be their most vocal opponent, but Driff was certainly their most dangerous.

"Remmar," Granger said, naming the next deceased elf in line. "A mother of three, she somehow still found time to bring over three dozen infants into the world through her work as a midwife." Somewhere between thirty and forty had fallen during the melee in Old Ev. They'd gone over the exact number in a briefing the night before, but Dash had quickly forgotten it. Remmar was the fifth laid to rest in the Origina.

Keighlan, sensing Dash's discomfort, squeezed his hand. The gesture somehow made him feel even more frustrated. He felt like he'd been kidnapped, like Keighlan and Lazzy and Gearix had tossed him in the trunk and sped off down the highway at Granger's behest.

"It'll be good to be involved again," Lazzy had argued vehemently during the five minutes Granger had given them to discuss his offer. "We've been on the sidelines for too long! Look what's happened without us!"

The women had nodded along like bobbleheads while Dash drained another beer. He'd wanted to slap Lazzy's stupid, smiling face. Like the four of them could've done anything about the Witch or Tallisker or Axzar. Dash had rather enjoyed his time on the sidelines. The responsibilities were few and far between and the view was pretty decent.

The crowd's attention suddenly diverted to a spot off to Dash's left. The energy in the park shifted, the air seeming to thicken. Roger Brooks looked ready to blast them all with the shotgun holstered at his hip. Dash kind of wanted him to try; at least then their little power struggle would be over quickly, one way or another, instead of dragging out for weeks as Granger had outlined. Roger's weapon remained safely stowed, however, and his mouth stayed shut. The Pintiri and his family and their two Gadukah bodyguards very pointedly walked right past Granger and the others to stand beside Driff. The battle lines were quite clearly drawn—just as the Council of Economics had said they would be.

"Harl," Granger said. "A loyal assistant to the last three Councils of Medicine, the man was also renowned for his skill as a painter and sculptor. Several of his beautiful pieces adorn my own office." Dash wondered how true that was. He had a really hard time picturing Granger as an art collector—or, truth be told, doing anything other than manipulating others for his own ends.

And so it went, as all elven funerals do. Granger named the deceased. A coffin sank to the bottom of the Origina. Dash found a new body part demanding to be itched. The spot where his palm met Keighlan's grew sweatier and stickier. Rinse, lather, repeat. After a while the eulogies all blended together. Were the deceased really all productive, beloved members of elven society as Granger described? Dash hadn't known any of them himself, so he couldn't say. Heck, he had several friends he would've had a difficult time writing a complimentary sentence about. That little nagging doubt threw the legitimacy of the entire affair into question.

Dash spaced out so badly that he missed most of the eulogies, but he snapped back to reality for the final three: Council of Agriculture Piney, Council of Medicine Chyve, and Council of Sorcery Aldern. Turns out Chyve spent her weekends volunteering at human orphanages, Aldern's pound cake recipe had been featured on a TV show, and Piney was Evitankari's backgammon champion—at least according to Granger.

"The waters of the Origina have taken our loved ones so that the great Evertree might blossom in their memory," the Council of Economics said as the final coffin sank. "They shall never be forgotten."

"They shall never be forgotten," those gathered repeated. Dash forgot to join in until the final word.

The crowd began to disperse, heading quickly for the exits. Despite Willowglen's beauty, most of Evitankari preferred to keep their visits rare and brief. The Evertree's park was associated with too many bad memories. Dash was less than thrilled that his new position as Council of Agriculture meant he'd have to spend more time in Willowglen as the park's primary caretaker. Although he planned to delegate the actual work to people more qualified, he'd have to visit often just to keep up appearances.

"That wasn't so bad," Keighlan whispered, squeezing his hand and smiling up at him.

He returned her squeeze. "Looks like the worst is yet to come." He nodded toward Roger Brooks and Driff, huddled together in intense whispered conversation.

"Granger says we've got them right where we want them," Keighlan said softly. "It's their two votes against our five." She'd been going on and on about the vote totals like they were some sort of magic shield. He didn't want to hear it anymore.

Surprisingly, it was the Pintiri's daughter who started the festivities. The blond young woman strolled right up to Dash and Keighlan and extended her hand. "Hello," she said brightly. "I don't believe we've met. I'm Samantha Brooks, the Pintiri's Chief of Staff."

Dash froze. Behind Samantha, Roger and Driff did the same. She'd clearly gone off whatever script the two men were desperately attempting to cobble together, but she'd also surprised the Lightning Club. Granger had insisted he'd be the focus of the opposition's attention. Dash had been counting on that. The less he had to be involved, the happier he'd be.

His wife came to the rescue. "Nice to meet you, dear," Keighlan said, gently shaking the offered hand. "I'm Council of Medicine Keighlan. This is my husband, Council of Agriculture Dash, and our friends, Council of War Lazzy, Council of Sorcery Gearix, and Council of Economics Granger."

Samantha's eyes lit up with shocked recognition for only a moment. "A pleasure. I was under the impression that the Council seats you all occupy were vacant."

Lazzy stepped in front of the others and quickly sized her up. "Until this morning, they were. The senior member of the Combined Council—that's Granger—has the power to fill empty Council positions on an interim basis until formal elections can be held."

Samantha nodded. "I see. Well, congratulations on your appointments. The Pintiri's office looks forward to working with you all until permanent Council members can be found." Out of the corner of his eye, Dash noticed the Pintiri's wife—whatever her name was—smiling at her daughter in approval.

Lazzy flinched. He'd been the most vocal about maneuvering to make his new position permanent. "I'm sure our time together will be both productive and educational for all involved."

"Lazzy..." Samantha mused, drumming her fingers on her thigh. "Is that short for something? Lazarus, perhaps?"

He shook his head and smiled. "An embellishment, for branding purposes. Are you a fan?"

"I was," she replied. "The story went a little off the rails in the final book."

Dash blanched and looked away. *Kid, you have no idea.*

— CHAPTER FIVE —

Team Brooks lingered in Willowglen as Granger's contingent departed. There was much work to do to get the new interim Council members up to speed, the Council of Economics explained, and Evitankari certainly wasn't going to run itself while their constituencies identified and elected replacements.

"It'll be about a month before the elections are even scheduled," Driff explained when Granger and the Lightning Club were out of earshot. "More than enough time for that shifter to accomplish whatever he's up to."

"You're sure Granger's a shifter?" Roger asked.

The elf nodded. "I killed the original myself. Security never recovered the body. Either that's a shifter or we've got a much bigger problem on our hands."

"So he's our focus, then," the Pintiri replied. "If we expose Granger, the whole thing falls apart."

Sam wasn't so sure about that, but she didn't have the information she needed to back up her position. Granger seemed like too obvious a target. "Why are they all named after characters from Lazarus Jones and the Lightning Club?" she asked, even though she was pretty sure she already knew the answer.

"Those *are* the characters from the Lazarus Jones and the Lightning Club," Hirace replied.

Sam sighed. Just as she'd thought. The physical resemblances gave it away. "Of course they are."

"The events in the books are mostly true," Hirace continued. "Lazzy, Dash, Gearix, and Keighlan really did save Evitankari from an evil sorcerer thirty years ago when they were teenagers."

"So they turned their adventures into a series of best-selling young adult novels?"

"Indeed they did."

"This place is so frickin' weird."

"You have no idea. I take it you read the entire series?"

"Several dozen times."

"Good, then you're up to speed," Driff said, cutting Hirace off. "Don't do that again, by the way."

"Don't do what again?" Sam snapped.

"That. Taking the lead in discussions before your father and I have finalized our approach."

"Aren't I supposed to be the bait?"

"Yes, but you will bait where and when we tell you."

She rolled her eyes. "I don't work for you. Dad?"

He rubbed his chin. "You can do that again. I'm going to encourage it, in fact." Beside him, Talora smiled warmly and nodded in agreement. Great.

"Thanks, boss," Sam said with a mock salute. "Driff, I'll try harder not to stomp all over your manhood next time I want to get something done."

The Council of Intelligence shook his head. "Let's not lose sight of who and what we're dealing with here," he said evenly. "Granger's a sentient puddle of ooze with undocumented powers of transformation. His new best friends are a quartet of beloved elven celebrities capable of exerting potentially incalculable influence on the local population. Each is competent and dangerous in his or her own unique way. Please think through your approach before engaging any of them—or anyone else in Evitankari, for that matter."

Driff had a good point, but Sam knew better than to admit it. "A good piece of bait draws direct attention to itself," she replied. "The more attention Granger and the Lightning Club pay me, the better it is for the two of you." She hated the idea, but for her father...she'd do whatever she had to. She hid her hands behind her back so the others wouldn't see them trembling.

"Just don't draw them too close until your father and I are ready to set the hook," Driff said.

"When will that be?" Roger asked.

"I'm working on it," the elf replied.

"Until then, I'll be extra careful," Sam said. "What's for lunch?"

Roger smiled mischievously. Sam had seen that grin before. It usually meant he'd done something that wasn't as amazingly clever as he thought it was. "You've got one more appointment first," Roger said. "Turn around."

Sam did as instructed. A little wooden boat had snuck up behind them and partially beached itself on the shore of the Origina. Woven together from thin strips of wood, it looked like it would have difficulty keeping its own meager weight afloat, let alone that of a fully grown adult. Its prow was twisted into the shape of a leaping fish with great big eyes. Samantha recognized the little boat immediately; it figured prominently in her father's retelling of his time in Evitankari, as did its master, the Evertree. She glanced across the pond at the massive willow and somehow managed to stifle a frustrated grunt.

"Thanks, Dad," she said carefully. "But don't we have work to do?"

"Who said this isn't work-related?" he asked with faux concern.

Conversing with a magical tree wasn't exactly at the top of Samantha Brooks's bucket list, and she wasn't too keen on leaving her father alone with Driff and Talora. One of the two was a devious, scheming, lying scumbag. The other was Driff.

Unfortunately for Samantha, she was out of excuses. She realized it would be best to just get this over with quickly. "All right," she replied. "I'll try not to be too long."

"Take all the time you need," Roger replied. Sam cringed as he wrapped his arm around Talora's waist, which made her want to get on that boat even less. It felt like she was being dropped off at her grandparents' for the weekend.

"Don't have too much fun without me," Samantha said as she turned and headed for the boat. She glared daggers at the sky, trying to forcibly evict from her mind the image of Driff plunging a knife into her father's back while Talora distracted him with a kiss. Not that she had any reason to suspect the two of them were in cahoots, but the obvious danger and her lack of understanding of her new situation sent her train of thought spiraling down into dark corners she never dreamed she'd have to consider. She would've been a terrible Chief of Staff and an even worse daughter if she hadn't worried about such things every now and then.

The interior of the Evertree's boat was, in a word, snug. There were no seats, so Sam sat on the deck. The seemingly fragile wood bent gently under her weight but held firm. She leaned forward and stretched, trying to find a slightly less uncomfortable position and failing miserably. *All that magic,* she thought, *and this is the best the Evertree can do?* Sure, the Origina was far too small to house a luxury yacht, but a vessel with a few cushions didn't seem like too much to ask for. And what would've been wrong about building a bridge?

The little boat launched itself into the water. Samantha studied her shoes, pointedly avoiding any possible glimpse of the mysterious Origina. She wondered what would happen if the boat capsized. Would the hungry pond swallow her right up and add her life to its collection? If she survived to reach the shore, would her soaked clothing carry important memories away from the Evertree? And what if she accidentally drank some? Would she inherit some of the pond's power? Would elven tradition require her to make amends to the descendants of those she'd inadvertently swallowed? She made a mental note to implement a very thorough on-boarding process for their next new hire.

The voyage across the Origina took only a minute or two, and then the boat gently ran itself aground on the Evertree's island. Samantha almost face-planted on the rocky shore as she leapt out. She collected herself and glanced back across the water. Hirace had taken a seat alone on the opposite shore, apparently awaiting her return. She was grateful someone would be there to escort her back to Merrowood, but ugh...*that guy*.

She parted the Evertree's fragile branches like a set of beaded curtains and stepped through. Although the sun's rays couldn't penetrate the willow's dense canopy, the area beneath its boughs was bright and vibrant. Half a dozen pixies flitted to and fro around the massive tree, lighting it all up in kaleidoscopic color.

"When does the DJ's set start?" Samantha asked, relying on snark to lessen her unease.

The gnarled old face in the Evertree's trunk smiled. "After close," it said in a deep, rumbling baritone. "VIP only. I can add you to the guest list if you like, Miss Brooks."

Sam's dumb human brain couldn't immediately process the Evertree's comprehension of her stupid joke. Trees aren't supposed to party, after all, or read, or watch TV, or browse the internet, or do any of the other things that would've provided the knowledge the Evertree would've required to formulate its response. Sam's skin began to crawl as understanding dawned. The Evertree was able to respond appropriately to her useless quip because of its access to the memories of deceased elves detailing the necessary experiences. That willow, she realized, had to be capable of conversing on any subject known to man and, undoubtedly, several hundred more mankind had no clue even existed. She took a few tentative steps forward to put just a little more distance between her back and the tree's drooping branches, just in case. She didn't want it sticking a twig in her ear and sucking out her miserable thirteenth birthday party or that time Timmy Landell broke up with her at the spring semiformal.

"I hear you have an affinity for history," the Evertree said.

"I dabble," she replied.

"It would seem you and I have a lot in common, then," it continued.

"That might be stretching it."

"Fair enough," the tree said, its tone still warm. "I thought we'd start at the beginning. The founding of Evitankari is one of my most requested memories. Please, place your hand on my trunk."

There was nothing Sam wanted to do less, except maybe make out with Hirace. "No thanks."

She was struck by how silly magic trees look when they're stunned. "I'm not sure I understand. The entirety of elven history is right here, at your disposal."

"Stupid human," one of the pixies added.

Sam stared down at the grass awkwardly. The Evertree seemed downright insulted, perhaps rightfully so. Its entire life centered around its one and only job, and she'd just sort of dismissed it. "I meant no offense," she croaked. Angering the willow seemed like a great way to end up trapped on its island or to get dumped overboard by its boat. "It's just...ah...I don't really trust all this magic." Telling the truth seemed like her best bet.

"Really stupid human," a different pixie chirped.

She ignored the little creature. "How does it work?" she asked. "Magic, I mean." Her lack of an answer to that question, after all, was the real crux of the problem.

The Evertree perked up. "All magic boils down to a transfer of energy. For example, a mage who wishes to create fire uses his own energy or that imbued upon him by a charm or potion to superheat the air around his fingertips. It's just physics."

Science had never been Samantha's strong suit, but the Evertree's explanation seemed a bit oversimplified. "If it's that simple, why can't humans do it?"

"Magic's a complex combination of quantum mechanics and biology humans simply aren't wired for. Your cells can't exert that sort of influence, and even if they could, you don't burn calories efficiently enough to generate any noticeable effects."

She supposed that made sense. "How does it work with what you do?"

"My magic tricks your nervous system into processing the memories of the deceased as if they're live experiences," the tree said proudly. "There's no sorcery like it anywhere in the world."

So you hijack people's brains, like some sort of virus infecting and manipulating a computer. She wondered if the tree ever demanded a credit card in exchange for returning control to the user. "That sounds...intense," she said carefully. Knowing more about how it all worked certainly hadn't made her more comfortable. "Maybe... we can work up to it?"

"I understand," the Evertree replied, although its drooping expression betrayed that it really didn't.

"So...tell me about you," Sam said with a smile. "What's your life like?"

"Ugh," one of the pixies grunted.

The willow looked down at its thick roots. "There's not really much to tell," it said sadly.

Whoops. She should've known better on that one.

"I've enjoyed meeting you, Sam, but there's one more piece of business we need to address before you go," the Evertree said matter-of-factly. "The memories of Council of Sorcery Aldern and Council of Medicine Chyve are missing."

It was Sam's turn to make a face. She'd just seen their coffins lowered into the Origina a few minutes ago, and their corpses had supposedly been inspected and identified just the night before. "How's that possible?" she asked.

"Most likely, their heads were removed."

Sam chewed on her bottom lip. Her next question felt pretty stupid, but she asked it anyway. "How do you know?"

"How do you know?" one of the pixies echoed mockingly. Samantha considered returning with a fly swatter, or maybe a vacuum cleaner.

"Because there's nothing there where Aldern and Chyve should be," the Evertree replied.

"So someone took their heads," Sam said, mystified to the point of borderline stupidity. "And that someone's got something to hide."

"Most likely."

"Unless there's some other benefit to owning those heads."

A pixie snorted. "Like what?"

Samantha blushed and shrugged. "Look, I've seen a lot of weird things in the last few days. Finding out some lunatic's just adding to the collection of severed heads on his mantel wouldn't surprise me in the least."

"Please communicate this information to the Pintiri," the Evertree said. The soft scratch of its boat grounding itself on the shore signaled Sam's dismissal. "I know not who's behind this crime, but I do know that your father's a man I can trust to solve it."

Sam added another entry on her Weird Things Dad Does Now list. "Will do," she said. "Thanks for the talk. See you again sometime?"

"When you're ready."

She nodded and turned to go, wishing that had gone better. The Evertree was one of her father's most trusted allies, and he was running a bit low on those. She'd have to make good on her offer to make a return visit. The tree's existence had to be a lonely one.

Thus began the tale of Samantha Brooks and the Case of the Missing Skulls. Although Sam hadn't yet constructed a firm motive for the crime, she had a pretty good idea who she needed to talk to first—and she decided not to waste any time confronting them.

— CHAPTER SIX —

Damn it, Dad! I'm not seducing the Pintiri's daughter just to help you keep tabs on her."

"Aubin!" Gearix snapped. "Language!"

"Why not?" Lazzy asked. "She's kind of cute. Don't you have a thing for blondes?"

Aubin's face flushed and he crossed his arms. "Seriously, Dad?"

Dash had never liked Lazzy's eldest son. He was the kind of kid who thought he could get through life just on good looks and his famous parents. It didn't help that Keighlan often doted on him like he was her own son.

"Just go on one or two dates," Lazzy said, his warm smile dripping with toxic sludge. "For your old man."

"No."

Dash took a sip of his scotch and water and leaned back in the puffy recliner he always claimed when he visited Lazzy's. Keighlan sat beside him on the chair's big arm, nursing her second red plastic cup of Gearix's supposedly world famous white sangria. On the other side of the sparsely appointed living room, Lazzy and his wife snuggled against each other on their big, plush couch. Aubin—tall, strapping, and blessed with his mother's freckles and red hair, but capable of wearing both better than she had at his age—glared at them all from the cased opening that led to the dining room.

"Aubin, deary," Keighlan slurred. "Why not? It might be fun. A little espionage. A little...romance." She raised her eyebrows a few times to punctuate her point. Dash kept a close eye on the stability of her drink.

"Aunt K, that's gross!"

"What's gross?"

His face went from red to purple. "She's...you know."

"No, Aubin, I don't know."

"She's...human."

Gearix gasped. "Aubin! Your father and I did not raise a racist!"

Yes you did, Dash thought as he knocked back the last of his scotch. Lazzy's plan to use his handsome son to scam information from the Pintiri's daughter was actually a pretty good idea, but it still made him feel super greasy.

"You're better than that, Auby," Keighlan chided.

No, he's not, Dash thought. *And neither are the rest of us.*

"You certainly are better than that, Aubin," Lazzy added. "Maybe even enough so to finally get that sword you've had your eye on. That Ox-Ordin, with the cobra etched into the blade."

Lazzy's son cocked his head, his interest obviously piqued. "With the optional comfort grip leather hilt?"

"Of course. A young man of such fine moral fortitude would deserve nothing less."

Aubin grunted and left the room. "I'll think about it," he called back over his shoulder.

Lazzy smiled and raised his glass of sangria in mock toast. "Got him." Dash wanted to punch his friend in the face. He realized that had been happening more and more in the last fifteen or so hours. He wasn't sure what to do about it.

The doorbell rang. Like everything else about Lazzy's house, Dash hated it. The thing was far too cheerful and perky, like it was announcing the arrival of a beloved, wholesome puppet on a children's TV show. Gearix excused herself and scurried off to answer it.

"You alright over there, Dash?" Lazzy asked, his concern so genuine it seemed oddly fake. "You've seemed a little off today."

Dash rubbed Keighlan's back and glanced at his knees. "I'm just trying to wrap my head around all this."

"What's there to think about?" Keighlan asked. "Granger's going to help us show Evitankari the truth about that sham of a Pintiri."

"And get the Lightning Club back in the spotlight in the process," Lazzy added.

"I get that," Dash replied. "But what's Granger get out of all this?"

Lazzy blinked, clearly not understanding. "What's it matter?"

From the adjoining hallway, Gearix cleared her throat. "Samantha Brooks would like a word with us."

Dash's breath caught in his throat. Embarrassed, he got up to fix himself another drink at the wet bar along the opposite wall. How had he become so afraid of an eighteen-year-old human with less than three days of experience living in Evitankari? There was no way she could possibly pose any sort of threat to them, but something about her just made him want to avoid her at all costs.

Gearix returned to her seat at Lazzy's side. Keighlan slid off the chair's arm and into Dash's empty seat and leaned forward, crossing her legs and trying to look serious and important but really looking like she might keel over at any moment. Samantha Brooks strolled into the living room and stopped just inside the cased opening. Behind Samantha, her Gadukah watchdog leaned against the wall and settled in to keep an eye on the proceedings.

"Miss Brooks," Lazzy chirped. "To what do we owe the pleasure?"

The girl's gaze flicked across each of them individually, finally settling on Keighlan. "We've got a problem. The Evertree has informed me that Aldern and Chyve's corpses were not deposited into the Origina intact. It has no access to their memories."

Gearix gasped. "Their heads..."

Dash reached past the bottle of cheap scotch from which Lazzy had poured his first round and went straight for the good stuff.

"Who would do such a thing?" Keighlan asked.

"Someone with something to hide, I'm thinking," Samantha said carefully. "Unless there's some other motive here the Evertree and I couldn't identify."

Dash poured himself three fingers, skipping the water this time.

"What possible use would a pair of severed heads be to anyone?" Keighlan asked.

Samantha shrugged. "I'm new. So's my father. That's why I came to you."

Stifling a snort, Dash drained a finger and a half with one swig and immediately replaced it with another splash from the bottle.

Lazzy patted his wife's thigh. "What about it, Council of Sorcery? Strange magic has always been your specialty."

"I don't know," Gearix said, shaking her head. "There are plenty of applications for the various pieces and parts involved, of course, but without more information I can't even begin to guess which we should be looking for."

"Trolls often use the eyes, ears, and tongues of their fallen enemies as soup ingredients," Keighlan slurred. Everyone ignored her.

"Hmmm," Samantha muttered. "Council of Agriculture, any thoughts?"

Dash almost spilled his scotch. "It's a head scratcher," he managed.

"Pun absolutely intended," Lazzy chirped. "Whatever's going on, it's a problem we won't solve from the safety of my living room. Was there anything else, Miss Brooks?"

She chewed on the inside of her cheek. "Keep the Council of Economics in the loop," she suggested. "If there's a market for celebrity heads, he may know about it. And I'm sure I don't need to remind you that this is a sensitive incident that should not be discussed outside of the Combined Council."

Lazzy pantomimed zipping his lips. "We will exercise the utmost in restraint."

"I know you will." She nodded politely. "The Pintiri's office will be in touch. Enjoy the rest of your day."

Samantha Brooks strolled out as if she owned the place and was just letting them use it. The Lightning Club studied their respective drinks until they heard the front door shut. Dash, meanwhile, also watched his companions out of the corners of his eyes, searching for some hint that one of them may have known more about the desecrated corpses of their predecessors than they were letting on. He seriously doubted any of them were involved, if only because they wouldn't have been able to keep their mouths shut about it.

Keighlan finally broke the silence. "We need to talk to Granger."

"No," Lazzy said. "We need to solve this one on our own."

"I don't know," Gearix replied. "Is this really something we want to stick our noses in?"

Lazzy smiled that obnoxiously handsome smile. "We're the Lightning Club. Sticking our noses in it is what we do."

— CHAPTER SEVEN —

Driff, needless to say, was not happy with Samantha's brief diversion to Lazzy's.

"You should've brought this information to us first," he said, just a hint of annoyance creeping into his mechanical voice. "Your father and I need to confer about such things before any action is taken."

The Council of Intelligence and the Pintiri were waiting for Sam on Merrowood's front porch when she and Hirace returned. Finding them there made Sam wonder if either one of them had an actual office or if all official Combined Council business took place wherever the required parties damn well pleased. For the record, there was an official Council Chamber, but it was typically only used for impressing outsiders or when a less formal meeting place couldn't be agreed upon.

"Job well done, Chief of Staff," Roger said happily. Beside him, Driff shook his head and rolled his eyes. "So if we're reasonably confident the Lightning Club wasn't involved in the theft, who does that leave as suspects?"

"The shifter masquerading as Council of Economics Granger, for one," Driff said. "And a large number of internal dissidents and outside actors."

"So we don't have a clue."

"Not yet, no. Once we're done here I'll investigate the morgue where the bodies were stored."

"Lazzy's surely got the same idea," Sam added.

"And this is why we meet to discuss new information before we volunteer it to people who might be our enemies," Driff said.

"Was it you?" Roger asked.

Driff rolled his eyes. "Yes. You got me."

"Had to ask."

"I know."

"Get to it then, Council of Intelligence," Roger said dramatically. "Meeting adjourned."

Driff glared at the Pintiri like he'd just caught him trying to steal his wallet. "That's not how this works." He shoved his hands in his pockets and stomped off Merrowood's front porch. "Although, this could be a golden opportunity."

Father and daughter frowned. "How so?" Roger asked.

Evil twinkled through Driff's piercing blue eyes. "Samantha, you were a big fan of the Lazarus Jones series, correct?"

"Correct. I read all the books and watched all the movies and I dressed up as Keighlan one Halloween, but I never went to any of the conventions or anything like that." Which was true only because her parents had told her no. Repeatedly.

The evil twinkling intensified. "Come with me."

— CHAPTER EIGHT —

Dash, meanwhile, was less than thrilled with his wife's outfit.

"We had to stop at home on our way to the morgue just so you could change into your old school uniform?" he asked as she trotted down the stairs and into their living room. Somehow he managed to swallow a snide comment about it not fitting so well anymore.

Keighlan smoothed the front of her black skirt and cocked her head at him. "Why not? This is just like the old days, D! The Lightning Club is on an investigation again!" She paused. "Finally."

Dash bit down hard on the tip of his tongue. Their situation was absolutely not like the old days—not that any of the others would know that—and he swore to himself right then and there that if it became anything at all like those old days he'd make a run for a nice ex-pat community somewhere warm.

"Too bad you threw out your uniform," Keighlan chirped, tapping his chest with the tip of her old black and yellow umbrella.

He reached down and buttoned the top button of her gray cardigan. "It's not raining."

She rolled her big blue eyes. "I know that, silly. It's for good luck. Remember when this very umbrella saved us from Kron the Withered's pet hellhounds?"

He pulled her close and kissed her forehead. "I'll never forget it," he lied. The truth was that he'd spent the last three decades trying to forget as much of their ordeal as he could.

Keighlan had always been well-attuned to her husband's moods, and this instance was no different. "Hey," she whispered. "This is going to be all right, Dash."

He hugged her tighter. "I'm just a little worried that we're rushing into something we don't fully understand."

Keighlan smiled brightly. "Since when has that ever stopped us?" She pulled away. "Oh. I get it. You're just jealous that I still look so great in my old school uniform!"

"Something like that."

They departed arm in arm, Keighlan twirling her lucky umbrella with her free hand. Lazzy and Gearix met them on the road at the edge of their property—also in their old uniforms. Dash considered excusing himself to go back inside for a shot of whiskey.

"That is quite obviously not academy-issued attire, young man," Lazzy said with a grin, aping Professor Cance's squeaky voice and precise diction. "Jeans and a hooded sweatshirt. You are an A-list cadet in training to become an elven sorcerer, not some human panhandling on the side of a highway."

Dash shrugged and tried not to gawk at Gearix. Her old uniform fit her like a glove. Dash sometimes still couldn't believe the gawky, awkward girl had grown up to be such a beautiful woman. Fucking Lazzy had all the luck.

"To the morgue we go!" Keighlan announced with an umbrella flourish before things could become awkward.

"So!" Lazzy said as the Lightning Club began their journey down the cobblestone street. "Theories?"

"Like Samantha Brooks suggested: someone's got something very important they're trying to hide from the Evertree," Gearix replied.

"Misdirection!" Keighlan offered. "Someone's looking to distract Evitankari's Combined Council from something more nefarious."

"The mortician's a freak with a severed head collection and he got greedy," Dash muttered.

"Gross!" Keighlan shrieked as she playfully slapped her husband in the butt with her umbrella.

"What about you, Laz? What do you think?" Gearix asked.

Lazzy shoved his hands in his pockets and looked somberly down at the ground. "I think Evitankari needs the Lightning Club."

Gearix rubbed his arm. "And that's exactly what Evitankari's going to get."

Dash wanted to vomit. *If the shit's really about to hit the fan*, he thought, *Evitankari certainly will need the Lightning Club—but the version from the books, not...this.*

Though the chatter continued, Dash blocked it out and refrained from participating. The others noticed, of course, but they were used to his occasional attempts to distance himself. Keighlan took his hand in hers at one point but otherwise they left him to his thoughts, of which there were surprisingly few. He'd been over it all so many times—not just their recent history, but their famous past as well—and sometimes he became so thoroughly frustrated that he shut right down. This was one of those times, and he let it take him because wasn't sure when he'd be able to afford another. For a few brief seconds he thought that maybe, rather than disconnect, he should enjoy the company of his three best friends, but...

That unfulfilled ellipsis was all the explanation Dash needed. He knew what it meant, and thinking about it enough to be able to better explain it was a task he'd long ago decided to avoid.

Evitankari's morgue, it turned out, was conveniently close to Willowglen, at the end of a narrow side street Dash was sure he'd walked past several dozen times without ever questioning where it led. Though he'd been to plenty of funerals, he'd never once realized that Evitankari even had a morgue, a fact that wasn't entirely odd among the general population. The elven capital's little pockets of civilization in the otherwise dense forest meant many important functional buildings were kept hidden. Dash's people loved keeping secrets, even from each other.

Of course, Council of Intelligence Driff and that damnable Samantha Brooks were waiting for them outside of the short, squat building. The latter clutched a notebook to her chest. "Watch yourselves," Dash muttered to his friends.

Lazzy looked back at him with a cocky smile. "Still afraid of teenage girls, Dash?"

Yes, he very much was. "Why's she here instead of her father?"

"The Pintiri's a busy man."

"The Pintiri's primarily a figurehead. Showing up just to look important is his primary responsibility."

"This one may not know that."

Keighlan squeezed her husband's hand. "Don't worry, D. I won't let the big, mean girl hurt you."

Dash resumed his previous bout of sulking.

"Dressed for the occasion, I see," Driff deadpanned.

"Same to you," Lazzy replied. "Do you ever take that coat off?"

The Council of Intelligence ignored him. "Welcome to the morgue. All staff save the director have been scheduled for further questioning and sent home. We'll have the place to ourselves."

Lazzy nodded. "Excellent. Let the investigation begin!"

Driff shook his head and turned toward the building. "Yes. Well. Follow me."

Samantha Brooks, who Dash was keeping a close eye on, fell into step beside Keighlan as they approached the morgue. At least one of the Gadukah had to be around somewhere, Dash knew. Not that he was thinking of trying anything. Or was he? Dash realized he'd gladly shove her down a well or a flight of stairs if given the opportunity. But no. Not here, and not yet. For now he was merely evaluating.

Keighlan—always the clever one—didn't miss her opportunity. "I take it you're a fan of the series?" she asked the girl. She'd sobered up enough that she only slurred every other word.

"I am," Samantha replied, just a hint of a blush creeping into her cheeks. "I've lost track of how many times I've watched the books or read the movies."

Keighlan laughed gently. "I believe you've got that backwards, my dear. It's always nice to meet a fan. Please, consider yourself an honorary member of the Lightning Club until the conclusion of our investigation."

Samantha's face lit up. "Th-thanks! Is that...is that your lucky umbrella?"

Just because it walks and talks like a starstruck fan doesn't mean it isn't secretly working to fuck us over, Dash thought. He made a mental note to remind Keighlan to be careful with the girl. If a bear had jumped out of the woods right then and there to maul Samantha Brooks, Dash would've left her to her fate and then toasted the beast's health later on.

Driff was about to open the morgue's double doors when someone on the other side did the job for him. A beady-eyed ghoul of an elf in a white smock burst forth and nearly sent the Council of Intelligence tumbling ass-over-teakettle back down the concrete stairs. "Hello everyone!" he shouted like a brightly colored puppet on a children's television show. "Welcome to the morgue!" Executive Director Cark. Devoted civil servant with over twenty-five years of experience in the funerary arts. Lives in his mother's basement with his collection of taxidermied cats.

The entrance hallway was impossibly white, bright, and sterile. Dash wrapped a protective arm around his wife as they all followed Cark inside. Fluorescent lights always fucked with Keighlan's equilibrium when she'd been day-drinking.

"This is the admissions area!" Cark chirped, his gray smile dripping with indescribable slime. "The recently deceased enter and exit the morgue through this corridor! They're identified to the best of our abilities, labeled, and examined one final time to ensure they've truly passed on!"

"'Identified to the best of your abilities,'" Lazzy repeated. "How confident are you in your team's identification of Council of Sorcery Aldern and Council of Medicine Chyve?"

"Supremely! I signed off on them myself!"

"Did you, now?"

Dash fought off a sigh.

"Of course! The Executive Director must sign off on the examination reports of all high-ranking elven officials!"

Lazzy considered that. "Good to know. Proceed."

"You got 'em, Laz," Dash mumbled under his breath. "Case closed." Keighlan jabbed him in the ribs.

Cark paused just outside the next set of double doors, which were trimmed in thick rubber and shut tight. He spread his long arms wide as if to envelop all of them in the sort of big, greasy hug usually employed by weird uncles or drunk stepmothers. "And now, the main event!" he crowed. "Beyond these humble doors lies the heart of the morgue—and, dare I say, the *coolest* part of our operation!" Dash found himself idly wondering if Cark paid for sex or if he just boned some sort of weird doll.

Driff turned to Gearix and Keighlan. "Your school uniforms may not be appropriate for this part. You'd be forgiven if you wish to remain here."

"Nonsense," Gearix snapped. "We've got a job to do." Beside her, Samantha Brooks smiled in admiration.

The Council of Intelligence shrugged and motioned for Cark to continue. The executive director snapped his fingers dramatically. Behind him, the double doors eased open. A blast of arctic air flooded the hallway. Keighlan pressed herself close to Dash for warmth. He shivered and wrapped his arms around her. This wasn't just some little chill; this was a midwinter's day in Antarctica, raw and unyielding.

"I present to you...cold storage!" Cark said with all the restraint of a carnival barker on crack cocaine. "Though our 'guests' typically don't linger long before their final journey to Willowglen, we still take all possible precautions to ensure their preservation. The decomposition of even a single synapse, after all, could steal an important memory from the Evertree's library."

Cold storage turned out to be a cavernous vault lined with floor-to-ceiling shelves for storing coffins. Two dozen examination tables were laid out in a precise circle around the room. In the center, a blue bonfire burned brightly in a stone pit.

"Cryogenic pyrokinetics," Gearix explained through chattering teeth. "Impressive."

Clearly fighting his body's attempts to shiver, Lazzy brushed past Executive Director Cark and strolled confidently into the vault. "I take it this is where Aldern and Chyve were kept between their deaths in Tash Square and their interment in Willowglen?"

"Precisely!" Cark replied. "The dearly deceased spent fewer than fifteen hours in our care!"

Gearix's green eyes were consumed by their black pupils as she summoned her magic. A shell of protective warmth rolled off her body in waves. She offered a hand to Samantha Brooks. The girl stared at it for a second, then carefully wrapped her fingers in Gearix's own. The spell spread across that physical connection to shield Samantha as well. Hand in hand, they followed Lazzy into cold storage.

"And where, exactly, were the bodies stored?" Gearix asked.

Cark pointed to a shelf just to the left of the front door. "Rack one, shelves one and two! We call it the VIP lounge!"

"It's been examined," Driff said. "Extensively." Lazzy climbed into the metal shelving anyway.

"And who has access to this space?" Gearix asked.

"A complex series of interwoven spells restricts cold storage access to only technicians scheduled for duty at the time!" Cark replied. "I adjust the wards myself as necessary!"

"Noted," Lazzy said as he clambered back out of the shelves. "Any other means of entry?"

Cark shook his head. "One way in, one way out! We take security very seriously around here!"

"And that door at the far end?"

"That's the bathroom!"

Lazzy nodded. "Of course." He stroked his chin in thought, searching for another angle. Dash wished his friend would just give it up. They weren't going to find anything here. Any evidence that had been left behind had surely been spirited away by Driff's investigators. This was all just for show, to give the illusion that Driff and the Pintiri were playing ball with the other members of the Combined Council, and Dash just wanted to get it over with and go home.

Lazzy, of course, wasn't having any of it. "And these tables? What are they for?"

"Final preparations!" Cark said. "One last physical examination, followed by the application of a chemical cocktail designed to further fight decomposition! Once that's complete, the subjects are sealed in their coffins and stored to await delivery to the Evertree!"

Dash couldn't see anything special about the cheap but solid looking slabs of slick metal. Lazzy stomped over to the nearest and ran his fingertip across the surface. Unsatisfied, he bent down to examine its underside. His eyes went briefly wide; something there had caught his attention. He made a big show of examining the remainder of the table and then moved to its neighbor.

Gearix didn't miss her cue. She steered Samantha Brooks back toward the main group. The others reflexively gathered around her. "So, let's review," she said carefully. "Following their deaths in Old Ev, Council of Sorcery Aldern and Council of Medicine Chyve were delivered to the morgue. After Executive Director Cark identified them in the corridor outside, each was placed on one of these tables and prepped for the funeral. They then spent the evening in their coffins, stored in that shelf by the door."

"Correct!" Cark replied. "I must say, you are just as astute as you are in the books!"

Gearix nodded politely. "Thank you, Executive Director Cark. It pleases me to know I'm able to live up to our ghostwriter's embellishments."

The two shared a warm laugh. Out of the corner of his eye, Dash saw Lazzy stick his smart phone underneath one of the examination tables and snap a picture.

"We're done here," Dash said. Keighlan shivered against him uncontrollably.

"Indeed," Lazzy added, returning to the group. "Thank you for your hospitality, Executive Director. We'll be in touch if we need anything else."

"Of course! The Lightning Club is always welcome in the morgue!" He caught himself. "I...uh...didn't mean it that way!"

Gearix giggled. "You'd better not have!" she said with a wink and a friendly squeeze of Samantha's hand.

Dash basically dragged Keighlan out of cold storage as quickly as his frozen bones would allow. "What a waste," he muttered.

She pinched his bottom rib. "These things take time, D. We didn't find Kron's lair in a day, you know."

Gearix let her warmth spell dissipate as she and Samantha crossed the threshold. "How'd you enjoy your first investigation with the Lightning Club?" she asked.

"It was interesting," Samantha replied. "You all seem to really know your stuff."

Dash wondered if she'd fit in his neighbor's wood chipper.

"We'll get to the bottom of this," Lazzy said sternly. "We have to. We're the Lightning Club, after all!"

Stepping outside into a gray, overcast day had never felt so good. Keighlan untangled herself from Dash and stretched. She looked back the way they came to make sure Cark hadn't followed them. "Something's off about that guy," she said softly.

"He works in a morgue," Driff replied stoically, as if that explained it all.

"Maybe," Lazzy said, scratching his chin once again. "Driff, I trust you'll keep us abreast of any developments in this case?"

"Of course. I should note that we've assigned extra screeners to examine the goods moving in and out of Port."

Keighlan pursed her lips. "I doubt the perpetrators will attempt to move the missing evidence out of Evitankari by conventional means."

"As do I," Driff replied, "but despite the lack of evidence here, it would be foolish to overestimate the intelligence of whichever party is behind this theft."

"Very good," Lazzy said. "Let's reconvene when we know more."

The Council of Intelligence nodded. "We'll take our leave of you, then."

"Yeah," Samantha said. "Who knows what Dad's up to without either of us there to keep an eye on him. Thanks again for letting me hang out with you all today."

Keighlan smiled happily. "Anytime, my dear. Give your family our best wishes."

The Lightning Club lingered outside the morgue as Driff and Samantha departed. Dash glared evil thoughts at the girl's back, trying to make her trip and fall through sheer force of will. It didn't work.

"Lazzy," Gearix said when they were finally alone. "What did you find?"

He whipped his smart phone out of his pocket to show them the picture he'd taken. There, scribed into the underside of the metal table, was a familiar spiraling rune. Keighlan gasped.

"That was on both of the tables I checked," Lazzy explained. "I suspect it was attached to the rest as well."

Dash swore. He hadn't seen that rune in almost three decades. He'd always hoped he'd never encounter it again.

"What's it mean?" Keighlan asked, shaking.

"It's Kron the Withered," Lazzy said gravely. "The bastard's back."

— CHAPTER NINE —

I demand a raise," Sam growled to her father and not-her-mother as she stomped onto the porch.

Roger, seated beside his supposed wife on the top step, crossed his eyes. "Did you have fun at work today, sweetie?"

She stopped dead in her tracks and took a deep breath in preparation to unleash a daughterly tirade of truly epic proportions. "Actually," she realized out loud, "I sort of did."

Roger clapped his hand on Talora's knee. "They grow up so fast!"

"Whatever," Sam replied in disgust. "Turns out confronting political rivals who were once your childhood heroes is exhausting work. Your Chief of Staff declares it nap time."

"You've earned it," Talora said to Samantha's indifferent back.

In the foyer, Ricky sat cross-legged in the middle of the floor with his nose buried in the pages of a thick comic book. His eyes darted up to his sister then went right back down to his reading. Sam didn't have the patience or the energy to ask him why he wasn't curled up somewhere more comfortable than atop that hard marble.

"Careful with that stuff, kid," she said on her way past. "Don't get attached."

He closed the book and looked down at his feet. "Sam, why would I want to savor the blood-curdling lamentations of my fallen enemies' widows?"

"Ask your father." At least now Sam knew he was getting all of his weird questions from comic books. Busy-body politicians everywhere would be vindicated if they ever found out. She resolved to find something more pleasant and educational for him to spend his time on. That sounded like a good task for Hirace.

Every step up the staircase was a trek to the top of Kilimanjaro. Sam hadn't felt so physically and emotionally drained since that time she'd foolishly tried out for the track team. She wondered if her fatigue was at least partially a side effect of Gearix's warmth spell—and she shuddered at the memory of that electric energy flowing into her flesh through the elven woman's soft palm. At the time, it'd seemed like an easy way to start getting over her fear of magic. Years ago, she would've relished the experience. Gearix! Her favorite character from her favorite series of books and movies! Casting a spell on her! Now that she knew magic was real, however, and understood what it could do and what it had done to her family...she felt stupid for letting someone she didn't know use it on her.

She banished the thought. She'd had an exceptionally long few days, and that was all. If Gearix had indeed sapped Sam's strength to power her spell, it was nothing a long nap wouldn't fix, especially on that absurdly comfortable bed Sam had claimed for herself.

Speaking of that bed, there was something waiting for her on top of it. At first glance she thought it was a paperback novel, but it turned out to just be a torn-off cover.

"Lazarus Jones and the Lightning Club: Steaming Pile of Horse Shit," she read out loud. Below the title, familiar illustrations of the teenage protagonists shoveled, swam in, and measured the titular heap of excrement. "Lovely," Sam muttered. She gingerly picked it up with the tips of her thumb and forefinger and turned it over. The other side was white and blank and completely unhelpful.

Sam debated running down to her father with whatever this was but then thought better of it. He had enough to worry about— assuming this wasn't just some dumb dad joke, of course, in which case she knew she'd hear about it soon enough. Something about that ruined book cover told her its origins were more sinister, however, although she couldn't for the life of her identify anyone with both a motive and the skills necessary to sneak such a thing into the Pintiri's home. Getting past her father probably wouldn't be that hard, but evading Walinda and whatever Gadukah were lurking around would be another story entirely. She supposed it could've been Driff, or maybe one of his subordinates, but he appeared to be playing nice for the moment.

And what was the message here? Was this commentary on the Lightning Club itself, or was it somehow tied to her work with the Council of Intelligence that afternoon? The latter seemed unlikely, simply given the timing. Was it a warning, then? Samantha already knew she needed to be incredibly careful around Lazzy and his friends, so what would be the point?

She stashed the cover in the nightstand, shut the door, killed the lights, and crawled under the warm, welcoming covers. One more dumb mystery in a city full of them, she thought. And if she'd learned anything from the Lazarus Jones series it was that mysteries were best solved after a good nap.

— CHAPTER TEN —

I don't know a Rot damned thing about agriculture, K," Dash said miserably. "Can we switch?"

Keighlan smiled at him from beside the kitchen island as she worked on his lunch. "You don't know a Rot damned thing about medicine, either." She punctuated that comment by dramatically slapping the top slice of bread down onto his turkey and cheese.

"Please don't hurt my sandwich," he deadpanned. "It's my first day working with the farmers. They'll laugh at me if I have a subpar lunch."

"Granger went over this," Keighlan continued as she fished in the drawer for a baggie. "It's all about branding and expectations. Lazzy's War because he's the big hero. Gearix is Sorcery because she's the smart, mysterious one. I'm Medicine because I'm compassionate and friendly. You're Agriculture because you're the sidekick and it's funny that way."

He crossed his arms and scowled. "That is not what Granger said."

Her smile got even brighter. Damn, that smile. Keighlan could only unleash its real power when she was off the sauce—it was also her first day meeting with her new constituents, so she'd forgone the morning mimosas—and at full strength it was like nothing else in Dash's universe. "True," she said. "But it's what he meant."

"So that line about saving the most important job for the most reliable member of the Lightning Club was bullshit?"

She stuck his sandwich into a plastic bag and zipped it tight with a flourish.

"I thought you were supposed to be the compassionate one."

Her features and posture softened. "I'm trying. I just want you to know exactly where you stand so you'll approach the task correctly."

He raised an eyebrow. "And how do I do that?"

Keighlan added the sandwich to the brown paper bag in which she'd previously packed an apple, a bag of chips, and a can of diet soda. Then she stomped across the linoleum and shoved it in his face. "Grab the job by the balls and prove the bastard wrong."

Dash gripped his wife by the hips and pulled her close. "I'll feed Evitankari like it's never been fed before." He kissed Keighlan's forehead, feeling genuinely better.

"Don't forget that you're in charge of the trash, too," she purred against his chest.

They walked to their first days of work together, hand in hand, until a fork in the road sent Dash toward the fields and Keighlan veering off in the general direction of the main hospital in Old Ev. As usual, they parted without saying goodbye. They'd never felt the need to. Dash clutched his bag lunch close and watched her until the thickening forest between them blocked his view. The symbolism bothered him, even though his brain usually didn't notice such things.

"This shit is making me way too introspective," he growled.

Still, he couldn't help wondering if his relationships with Keighlan and Lazzy and Gearix would be the same after whatever it was they'd gotten themselves into finally came to an end. In a way, their assignments to their various new constituencies felt like a wedge being gently maneuvered between them in preparation for a hammer strike that would violently drive them apart. Perhaps Granger viewed the Lightning Club as a threat as much as he saw them as useful allies and had set them up to fragment when they were no longer necessary. It was a worrisome thought to be sure, and it reminded him just how little he knew about the Council of Economics. Granger had always been one of the more mysterious members of the Council, seemingly content to quietly go about his business away from the spotlight commanded by the legendary Council of Sorcery Aldern and the bombastic Council of War Pike. He hadn't been the senior member of the Combined Council back then, of course, and the deaths of most of Evitankari's other leaders had left a massive power vacuum just waiting to be filled by whoever decided to step up. Maybe Granger was just a concerned public servant nobly filling the void left by his departed peers.

Dash wasn't that naïve.

The road dipped down into a sprawling valley. The city's dense forests gave way to endless flat farmland speckled here and there with homesteads, barns, silos, and other structures Dash couldn't name. *A whole lot of nothing*, he thought before he corrected himself. The population density of Evitankari's agricultural areas wasn't all that different from many of its residential neighborhoods; the lack of trees simply made the empty space much more obvious. Dash hadn't visited since a class field trip a couple months before Kron the Withered's rune had begun appearing on the chalkboard.

Granger's directions were to go through the first gate on the right, walk to the main barn, and ask for Lesryn. Easy enough, but worrying in the lack of detail. Dash found the simple wooden gate about a hundred paces into the valley. Old but obviously well-maintained, it gave easily at his touch and opened soundlessly, admitting the new Council of Agriculture onto a narrow dirt path cutting through an empty pasture. The main barn waited for him in the distance like like a tombstone.

The walk down that path couldn't have been lonelier. Dash had spent the vast majority of his life sheltered among the elven capital's forests. Without a canopy to dilute the sun and trunks and branches to slow the breeze, he felt exposed and vulnerable. Dread welled up so strongly in his chest he almost turned around. After all, if the farmers decided they couldn't stand the thought of deferring to Dash as their temporary leader and representative, well...he was pretty boned. It wouldn't be hard to "lose" an interim Council of Agriculture out there.

Pride—combined with the knowledge that he was probably being really silly—pushed him onward. After all, he was the Dash, reliable sidekick of the real-life inspiration for Lazarus Jones, and his exploits against Kron the Withered were famous the world over! Sure, the story had been sort of embellished, but still! Neither unhappy farmers nor a minor case of agoraphobia nor even the horrible Samantha Brooks herself could stop him!

"Rot, now I sound like Lazzy and the rest of 'em," he muttered. Ashamed, he shoved his free hand deep into his pocket and hugged his lunch close.

He was about halfway to the barn when he realized he was being watched. The voyeur in question leaned forward over an inexplicably positioned length of fencing just before the barn that may have been constructed there purely for his convenience. Tall and rail thin, his piercing blue eyes somehow seemed to be the largest part of his body. A pair of denim overalls hung from his bony shoulders as if attempting to flee to the nearest laundromat for some much-needed attention. His head was too big for his neck, his callused hands were far to filthy to eat with, and his mullet was too long and too greasy to plausibly exist outside of the continental United States.

"Hello there," Dash called out politely when he'd closed to what he thought was an appropriate distance. Keighlan had a tendency to collapse on the couch to watch old Westerns after one too many cocktails, and everything Dash knew about visiting someone else's homestead he'd learned from Clint and the Duke while snuggling with his wife. He was pretty sure he'd done it right.

The man leaning on the fence gave no indication he'd even heard Dash. He continued staring straight ahead at the newcomer while chewing on a stalk of wheat or hay or pineapple or whatever the hell that was. Dash had no clue. He paid a gardener to mow the lawn twice a month.

Finally they were too close to one another for Dash to let the man's lack of a response slide. "Hi," he said, more sharply than he intended. "I'm Dash, the interim Council of Agriculture. I'm looking for Lesryn."

The man chomped down on his chew toy so hard Dash expected it to burst. "Ah," he said, his deep baritone sputtering like an old engine struggling to turn over. "Yeah."

Dash waited for more, but it never came. "Alright," he said as he hurried past. "Nice to meet you." It wasn't, but being polite to his new constituents seemed wise.

He wound up walking three quarters of the way around the barn before he found its entrance. The big sliding door was just barely cracked, hiding the interior. Seated on a bale of hay beside that door was a short, sturdy young woman in jeans and a flannel shirt.

Lesryn. Popular rising star in Agriculture's leadership structure. Suspicious lack of identified flaws or bad habits.

A bright smile burst to life across her round face. "You must be Dash!" she said warmly, setting him immediately at ease. "Welcome to farm country, Council!" The dusting of freckles across her nose and cheeks reminded him of Gearix.

"Thanks for having me," he replied. "I look forward to serving as your representative."

She burst up to her feet, seemingly propelled by an explosion of gentle laughter. "Somebody's been practicing his pleasantries!"

Dash normally wasn't impressed by overly effervescent cuteness, but he wanted to tuck Lesryn under his arm and bring her home to show Keighlan. "Ready for your first day?" she asked.

"I am now," he replied happily, letting some of the old, cocksure Dash slip through his jaded adult façade. If the rest of his constituents were more like Lesryn than like that guy back on the fence he might actually come to enjoy the job. Emboldened, he jerked his head back toward the direction of the main road. "I think I caught the welcoming committee off guard."

Lesryn's smile somehow got even bigger. "Don't mind Corken! He's really a big teddy bear once he gets used to you."

"I could tell."

She nodded. "Now that introductions are taken care of...let's get to work."

"Let's."

She slid the barn door open just wide enough to step through. Dash followed her inside. He wondered what they'd be working on first. Drought mitigation strategies? Livestock disease management? A top secret project to make Willowglen's famously green grass even greener? Perhaps a last-ditch effort to save an important wheat field from a particularly ugly and voracious flock of locusts? The possibilities were oddly exciting. Dash felt like he was once again sixteen and ready to save the world—or at least Evitankari's pantries.

Inside the barn, however, he found a classroom. Five rows of six wooden desks hummed with the activity of unattended ten-year-olds. Dust and hay exploded up from the dirty concrete floor as the surprised students scurried back into their seats and readied their notebooks. The class was silent and ready when Dash and Lesryn reached the podium up front.

"Good morning, everyone!" Lesryn chirped.

"Good morning, Professor L!" the kids replied in ragged unison.

"We've got a guest today! This is Interim Council of Agriculture Dash!"

"Good morning, Interim Council of Agriculture Dash!"

"Hi," he sputtered, clutching his lunch bag so tightly he worried it might burst. As far as Dash was concerned, being stuck in front of a crowd was the only thing in life worse than being surrounded by children. He wished he had a beer to awkwardly sip.

Lesryn stepped behind him and pulled down a projector screen dangling from the barn's thick rafters. "Your seat's in the back corner, next to Nitch."

Dash bit back a rather un-Council-like "M-m-m-my seat?" and shifted uncomfortably. He supposed it made sense that he'd need a bit of training before stepping into his full responsibilities, but was shoving him into a classroom full of brats the best way to get him up to speed?

Lesryn cleared her throat. Dash took the hint, bowed his head, and shuffled off to his seat. Causing a scene would get him nowhere. Keighlan's earlier words of encouragement echoed in his head. If he stuck it out, worked hard, and put in the time to prove himself, the farmers would accept him eventually. *Rot*, he thought, *I sound like Lazzy*. He *hated* sounding like Lazzy.

When Dash looked up a few furtive strides later he found Nitch staring him down. Sure, all the kids were watching him, but the pressure of that scrawny ginger's laser-sharp gaze overwhelmed the rest. It was like being locked onto by a freckled, bucktoothed missile. Dash offered the kid a little wave as he sat down in the desk to his right. Nitch responded by pushing a bubble of snot out of his nostril and remaining unnervingly still when it finally popped and dribbled down his upper lip.

Lesryn confidently strode to the back of the classroom, taking up a position behind a clunky old projector on a metal cart. She magically deactivated the room's fluorescent lights with a snap of her fingers. "Okay, class!" she declared as the projector sputtered to what could only loosely be described as life. "You know the drill!"

The first slide thunked into place.

"Cow!" twenty-nine ten-year-olds shrieked at the black and white photo on the screen.

"And what does the cow say?" Lesryn asked.

"Moooooooooooooooooo!"

Dash sunk down low in his seat, wishing he could melt into the floor. Nitch, who was still staring, blew another snot bubble his way.

"Chicken!"

Dash glared at the rooster onscreen, trying—and failing—to whip up a snappy one-liner about how it wasn't the only giant cock in the room.

— CHAPTER ELEVEN —

In what she'd come to think of as her first life, Samantha Brooks had always enjoyed surprises. Like Winston, the puppy her father had brought home one night when she was four. Or the party her friends had thrown her at the water park for her sweet sixteen. Or even just finding a prize at the bottom of the cereal box. Even pop quizzes and unannounced fire drills had given her a little thrill. She was smart, and so she usually had a pretty good idea how things were going to go. Anything that threw a small twist into her assumptive future was a welcome change as long as it didn't bring with it anything too terrible.

Walking through the streets of Evitankari, blindfolded, toward something her father had described as "frickin' awesome" in his best dorky dad tone, however, felt like the wrong sort of surprise. She had no clue what her father was up to and she doubted it was going to end well. At least attempting to puzzle out his intentions took her mind off the Case of the Missing Heads for a while. What in Evitankari would Roger Brooks deem cool enough to deserve his beloved daughter's attention? Something weird and magical, no doubt, which made Sam wonder if her father had somehow missed the less-than-subtle hints she'd dropped about her distrust of such things. She certainly didn't expect Evitankari to have a normal old water park.

Not long after their departure from Merrowood, a perky voice dragged a sheet of 80-grit sandpaper across Sam's soul. "Here's that other thing you asked for, Pintiri!" Hiperian Battlemage First Class Ivree. One of the most powerful sorcerers in Evitankari. Fiery personality and a penchant for mischief that would've landed her in jail years ago if she weren't a member of the Gadukah.

"Thanks," Roger said awkwardly.

"What other thing?" Sam asked. The blindfold was tight and dark and smelled oddly of patchouli. Her father squeezed her hand in response but offered no further explanation.

"I think you need to stick it in further," Talora said helpfully.

Sam's mind went to places her tongue wasn't allowed. "Oh, come on!"

Roger hissed in pain. "I think that did it."

"Your Chief of Staff needs to be kept in the loop."

"What number am I thinking of?" Hirace asked.

"Seven," Sam guessed.

"One thousand, four hundred and twenty-five," Roger replied matter-of-factly.

The elf didn't respond verbally. Perhaps there was a nod or a shake of the head; Sam would never know. She growled, but none of the others acknowledged her. The authority of the Chief of Staff position, it seemed, was under attack. She bit back a laundry list of snide comments. Her father had never been good at keeping a secret. Whatever he'd just done to himself with the Gadukah's assistance would come out soon enough.

And so they walked. It felt like a reasonably sunny day, although they'd blindfolded Samantha in the foyer and she hadn't looked out the windows that morning so maybe she was imagining that part. She was glad Walinda had provided sneakers with thick soles. Evitankari's cobblestones were pretty but they would've been hell in flats or heels. Samantha counted their steps, their lefts, and their rights, and she came to the conclusion that they were journeying to a part of the city she hadn't visited before. Her mind flickered through a mental slideshow of all the obnoxious things that might be lurking in the city's pocket neighborhoods. Mimes trapped in real invisible boxes. Hirace's favorite open mic night. An expensive organic grocery store with an over-designed concept and stupidly loud self-checkout.

"Where do elves do their food shopping?" she asked. The others continued to ignore her. She wondered if the Lightning Club needed a Chief of Staff.

Finally her father brought her to a stop. The ground under her feet was softer than the dense cobblestones of the elven roads. She really hoped she was standing in normal grass and not something weird.

Roger sighed dramatically, clearly pleased with himself. "You're gonna love this."

"Great." Sam sniffed the air carefully, searching for clues. "But what was that other thing?" She couldn't help herself.

"Don't worry about that. Your mother was a huge help, by the way. There were three of these and I couldn't decide which to choose. She said this one felt the most like you."

Sam's blood pressure spiked into the stratosphere but her mouth successfully clamped down on her enraged tongue. There would come a time, she knew, when loudly denouncing not-her-mother would become an actual good idea and not merely a satisfying one. Blindfolded in the middle of who-knows-where among people supposedly doing something nice for her was not that time, no matter how desperately she wanted to protest that Talora didn't know a single damn thing about her and as such couldn't possibly identify anything that "felt" like Samantha Brooks. She forced herself to relax and hoped no one noticed. "Thanks," she croaked.

"You're welcome," Talora replied warmly.

Roger removed the dark cloth covering his daughter's eyes. Sam blinked against the daylight a few times before her vision adjusted. "That's a house."

"A one-and-a-half story, eleven hundred square foot cape-style home built in 1947," Roger replied. "Two beds, one bath, working fireplace, farmhouse sink, brick patio in the back. Fully furnished." He paused for effect. "And there's chocolate ice cream in the freezer."

Sam blinked again, slower this time, as she processed all the details. The little blue and white house was super cute and super New England. She'd passed three or four just like it on her way to and from school every day, but none of them had been quite this nice. The paint was fresh, the roof was new, and the window boxes were bursting with tiny pink and purple flowers. A proud bronze rooster watched over it all from a weathervane atop the roof. The house was perfectly symmetrical and perfectly kept and perfectly...perfect. Only later would Sam reflect on how odd it was that Talora—a woman who'd only known her for a scant few days and who absolutely was *not* her mother—had chosen it specifically for her and that she'd done an amazing job.

"This is my house?"

"Yes," Roger beamed. "Merrowood's nice and all, but you're an adult and you should have a home of your own. Especially given what happened to the last one."

Samantha struggled with his last sentence for a few seconds before she grasped its meaning. She'd been so busy with and worried about life in Evitankari that she'd forgotten about the fire that had consumed the Brooks family home the night Roger discovered the Ether. A wave of guilt and sadness washed through her. She'd lived in that house almost her entire life and she didn't even know how much of it was still standing or if anything inside of it had survived. That felt like a huge betrayal.

Ivree thrust a set of keys into her face and jangled them obnoxiously. "Want to take her for a spin?"

That snapped Sam out of her reverie. "Of course I do," she said as she snatched the keys out of the short woman's fingers.

The front door unlocked smoothly with a satisfying click. Sam's heart pounded as she stepped into the front hallway. There was an empty shoe rack on her left, a row of wooden coat hooks on the wall to her right, and just enough room in between for a thin blue carpet that ran off toward the kitchen at the far end of the house. Sam instinctively took her sneakers off; this was her house, damn it, and it was going to stay immaculate for as long as she could keep it that way.

A few strides later, cased openings on either side led to a living room and a dining room. She decided to explore the former first, a tight, homey space bursting with plush furniture, bright wood, and simple electronics—a fantastic change of pace from the garish den the former Pintiri had left behind in Merrowood. She couldn't wait to fall asleep on that couch while watching a movie.

Samantha's father sauntered in behind her and pointed at the painting hanging above the red brick mantle. "I picked that out myself," he said with exaggerated arrogance.

She leaned back, crossed her arms, raised one hand to her chin, and pretended to study what she could only describe as a lovable atrocity. "Hmm. Yes. A bespectacled basset hound tending bar for a variety of other dogs as a lone feline stares inside longingly through a window. It...speaks to me." She loved it.

"I knew it would."

Sam noticed the two Gadukah and Talora watching from the hallway. A concerning thought pierced her excitement. "Hold on," she said. "This is all part of that 'being bait' thing, isn't it?"

Her father shifted uncomfortably. "Sort of, but...not to your mother and me."

"Driff!" Sam snapped. "Show yourself!" He didn't.

"He's not here," Roger said.

"He's always here. Driff!"

"Seriously, he's not here."

Sam chewed on her lip, unconvinced but out of arguments. "Fine. Thank you, by the way."

Roger's smile lit up the room. "You're welcome. Oh, there's one more thing." He shoved his hand into his pants pocket and fished out a tiny clay pendant on a thin black string. "Remember when we talked about finding you some sort of protection?"

She eyed the pendant warily. It reminded her of a similar piece of jewelry she'd bought during a family beach vacation when she was thirteen or fourteen. She'd worn it everywhere until an unfortunate mishap with an eleventh grade biology textbook shattered it into a dozen pieces. Where the face of the original was carved with the crooked, amateurish image of a sailboat, this one featured a precise reproduction of her newly acquired house. She didn't dare guess what feats of magical weirdness it could perform, and she didn't really want to know. "Can I just have a gun?"

Ivree cackled from the hallway. Roger shook his head. "No."

"Why not?"

Hirace stepped into the room beside her father. "Statistically speaking, the sort of firearm you could easily conceal would be useless against the vast majority of likely threats," he said helpfully.

Sam scowled, once again annoyed by the elf's mere presence. "So get me one that isn't statistically useless. A really big one. Or two."

"No weapons until you're old enough to rent a car," Roger said. "That's final."

She took the pendant and turned it over in her hands. It was heavier than it looked, and strangely warm. "How's it work?"

"It's a transpoint—the one-way sort," Hirace replied. "It's entangled to a brick on the side of your fireplace. Touch the pendant, think yourself home...and you'll end up right here."

Samantha chewed on that for a second. "But what if the danger's here, in the house?"

As if on cue, the doorbell rang. Roger almost leapt out of his shoes in surprise. "Hirace, if you would?"

The elf departed to deal with their unexpected visitor. Sam chuckled to herself and shook her head. "Didn't think that part through, did you?"

"Just...don't open the door for strangers."

"Thanks, Dad."

Hirace returned. "It's Granger."

"Tell him nobody's home," Sam replied quickly. "I'll close the curtains. Dad, kill the lights."

Roger sighed. "If only. I can't not speak to the shifter illegally occupying one of Evitankari's most important governmental positions."

"Outside, then," Sam insisted. She slipped the pendant on. "I don't want that thing in my house."

One by one, they filtered back outside to confront Granger. The two Gadukah exited first and took up positions beside and slightly behind the Council of Economics. Talora and Samantha glared daggers through him as they stepped out into the yard. Finally, Roger emerged with his hand resting suggestively on the butt of his holstered shotgun.

"You've got me surrounded, Pintiri," the shifter said jovially. "I brought a casserole." He offered Samantha a rectangular glass dish covered in aluminum foil. She made no move to accept it.

"How'd you know we were here?" Roger asked.

"I'm the Council of Economics!" Granger paused for dramatic effect. "And it's not every day the Pintiri purchases additional property in Evitankari."

Sam looked to her father. "How did you pay for this?"

Roger shrugged. "A brief rider in the budgeting act of 1464 granted the Pintiri's office access to a rather large discretionary fund. Strong returns from a series of wise investments—primarily in manufacturing and rare minerals—has resulted in a perpetually growing nest egg that should support the Pintiri's efforts for generations. Expenditures over a certain amount must be approved by the Combined Council, however."

Samantha's eyes narrowed in suspicion. "Someone's been reading up."

"I assure you it was a legit purchase, Miss Brooks," Granger added. "Your new home is not something I or anyone else can use against you."

"Why are you here, then?" Talora asked.

"It's time to clear the air between us. I assume you've concluded by now that I am not, in fact, Council of Economics Granger."

"You don't say," Roger deadpanned.

"And you must have some idea as to why I've assumed this Rot-awful form."

"I assume it's to further destabilize Evitankari while we're still reeling from the Witch's attack."

"You assume incorrectly, Pintiri. I am here to ensure Evitankari's survival, not to hasten its demise."

"This is the face I make when I know I'm hearing a load of horseshit," Roger growled. Sam knew it to also be the face he made when falling asleep on the couch during the seventh inning of a ballgame, but she decided not to embarrass her father in front of his friends.

Granger shook his head. "My kind has found a rather comfortable niche in the shadows of the current world order. A strong elven state is rather important to the security of our position. We have no desire to take over. As I'm sure you've noticed, those on top quickly become the targets of society's more...disruptive elements. Infiltrating the Combined Council is a rather extreme step, but one we deemed necessary. Think for a moment about the composition of the Council following the battle in Tash Square."

Roger scratched his head. "Driff kind of sucks and Aeric's in jail, but I'm an all right guy."

Realization dawned on Samantha. "All three of you have ties to the Witch. They're not worried about us. They're worried about her."

"Exactly," Granger replied. "And don't forget that one of the Witch's protégés has the Pintiri's ear." Talora cocked her head, considering.

"Fine. You've certainly got reason to worry about the Witch's continued influence," Sam continued. "Assuming the guise of the senior member of the Council and using that power to appoint the Lightning Club to temporarily fill the empty positions allowed you to create an unbreakable voting bloc that can stymie anything we might try to push through."

Granger smiled. "You've chosen a very capable Chief of Staff, Pintiri."

"Nepotism at its best!" Roger declared enthusiastically. "You know how I chose my minions. How'd you pick out yours?"

That question had been bothering Samantha for days and she wished she'd thought to ask it first. Oh well. She could let her father have one, every now and then.

"The Lightning Club are popular, recognizable, and known to be more than capable. They're also an impartial choice that candidates seeking permanent election to their positions will feel no reason to be threatened by."

"Dash is going to make a terrible Council of Agriculture," Sam said, calling on her knowledge of the book series. "And there's no way he'll want the job long-term."

"Plus, the appointment of such a famous quartet distracts from Granger's own ascension to the senior seat. I loathe unnecessary attention, believe it or not."

Sam's mind kept spinning. There was something about the Lightning Club the shifter had left unsaid—she was sure of it. That strange book cover she'd discovered on her bedspread had hinted that their official story was missing a few details. Were the shifters somehow in possession of that information? Could it be used to manipulate Lazzy and the others?

"So," Roger said, "where do we go from here?"

The shifter looked to Samantha. "First off, you really ought to take this casserole. Granger's widow is a lovely woman and an excellent cook."

"Truth," Ivree interjected. "I'll take it if you don't want it."

Sam gave in and accepted the dish. "We can split it." But she was definitely going to make Ivree try it first, just in case. "Please extend my thanks to the chef."

"She will be most pleased," Granger replied with the most authentic smile Sam had seen him deploy. "Now, as for less important matters...I ask only that you allow me to serve in my current role until after the elections to install permanent replacements for the Councils of Sorcery, Medicine, Agriculture, and War."

Samantha was just beginning to process the ramifications of Granger's request when her father suddenly took the lead. "Deal," he declared. Ivree's left eyebrow almost launched itself into the stratosphere.

"Although I am supremely confident in my negotiating abilities, that was too easy," Granger said suspiciously.

"In return, you shall see to it that the Lightning Club involves my Chief of Staff in all activities related to their investigation."

"Consider it done."

Sam struggled to process what was happening as the two men cordially shook hands. Why had her father been so quick to cut a deal with a known foreign agent that could easily put his beloved daughter in harm's way? Why leave the shifter in a position where he could potentially do incalculable damage to Evitankari? Sam tried to exchange nervous glances with Ivree and Hirace but neither seemed even slightly perturbed. She didn't think to look to Talora. Rather than potentially undermine her father, Sam decided to keep her objections to herself for the moment.

Granger departed immediately. When the shifter was out of earshot, Sam handed Ivree the casserole so she could punch Roger hard in the shoulder. "Dad," she hissed, "what the hell?"

Driff materialized beside them. "Interesting move," he mused. "Allowing the shifter to maintain its current guise is a risk, but at least we know where it is."

"Nobody asked you," Samantha said. "And if you were in my house you'd better have taken your shoes off."

"We've also successfully planted an agent in their operation, just in case Granger's not on the up and up," Roger added proudly. "You're gonna do great, Sam."

She glowered at him, taking a few moments to carefully consider her response. "You're not invited for casserole tonight."

— CHAPTER TWELVE —

It took a couple of days, but Gearix found the lead the Lightning Club needed.

"Balacath works the nightshift in Port," she said triumphantly. "He's a low-level inventory inspector."

Dash didn't see how that was relevant. "Why would we want to bother our old classmate?"

Lazzy looked at him quizzically. "Have you already forgotten the hell he put us all through? He's not just our classmate: he was Kron the Withered's apprentice!"

And he'd been royally fucked in the head at the time—a fact Dash had long ago given up trying to drive through Lazzy's thick skull. In spite of his alliance with Kron the Withered, Balacath had never really been a bad guy. He just had an unfortunate face. And a famously trashy family. And body odor that could clear a room. And an ill-advised penchant for wearing suspenders and a bowtie. Balacath had been an easy target, and the merciless teasing and pranking that had driven him to the evil sorcerer couldn't possibly have been avoided.

Dash didn't bother looking up from the television. "I'll never forget what Balacath did to us," he said half-heartedly. The ensuing dramatic pause served as perfect cover for the time he needed to figure out a decent reason to avoid bothering their old classmate. He'd spent an exhausting day making construction paper llamas and learning to identify various types of shovels and he intended to spend the next several hours staring blankly at a basketball game. "This seems like a dead end. If Kron really is back, he'd be taking a pretty big risk by working with any of his known associates."

"If you've got a better idea for how we can make some actual progress with this case, I'd love to hear it," Gearix said.

Keighlan snatched the remote from the arm of Dash's recliner and used it to turn the TV off. "Dash, come on," she said with that knowing look that always made him squirm. While Dash was glad she'd seriously curtailed her drinking because of the case, Keighlan's sobriety made it a lot harder for him to get away with what she'd started calling his "usual bullshit."

"Fine," he said, hauling himself up. "But what do we do about the Brooks girl? Granger said we're supposed to include her in our investigations."

"Leave that to me," Lazzy said with a smarmy smile. Gearix scowled and smacked him in the back of the head.

They met Samantha in Old Ev an hour later, outside Nonny's Bookshop. The Pintiri had sent one of his Gadukah—former Council of War Pike's nephew, Dash was pretty sure—along as her escort. Hands cupped around her eyes, Samantha leaned right up against the rickety wooden shop's hazy window to get a better look at the nonsensical maze of academy supplies inside. Dash and Lazzy had famously first met their wives among those confusing stacks when they'd accidentally toppled a six-foot-tall pile of alchemy textbooks right on top of the girls. It was a place near and dear to the Lightning Club and their fans.

Lazzy took the lead while Dash tried to hide behind Keighlan and Gearix. Hirace, leaning on the metal pipe railing beside Samantha, watched them all with a practiced eye, looking carefully for any sign of a threat. The Gadukah had always sort of given Dash the creeps. Deadly, highly trained commandos that answered not to Evitankari's government but only to a single man within it were not the sort of people he preferred to associate with. They were a haughty, overconfident bunch, empowered by their position, and the previous Pintiri had filled the squad with quite an odd cast of characters. Dash was glad Roger hadn't sent that Ivree maniac.

"Evening," Lazzy said to Samantha. "Bet you never thought you'd get to visit this place."

She glanced back over her shoulder at the rickety brick building where the Lightning Club had done their school shopping. "Too bad it's closed," she replied, the disappointment obvious in her voice. "But thank you for showing me where it is. I'll have to come back during the day to meet Nonny sometime."

"He's always thrilled to meet a fan," Lazzy replied. "Speaking of making new friends, allow me to introduce you to my son, Aubin."

Dash cringed as the boy strode forward. Lazzy's plan to get to Samantha Brooks using his handsome son couldn't have possibly been more transparent. She was a big fan of the fictional Lightning Club, sure, but she wasn't stupid. Dash expected her to immediately recognize the ploy, crack a moderately funny one-liner, and tear Aubin's testicles off.

Instead...she blushed. "Nice to meet you," she said softly as she shook his hand.

"A pleasure," Aubin replied smoothly, flashing the boyish smile he'd inherited from his father.

What passed between them when their palms touched wasn't a spark so much as a full-fledged electrical storm. Samantha almost seemed to shrink. It was weird and awkward and off-putting and forced Dash to wonder if maybe—just maybe—the Pintiri's eldest child wasn't actually as terrifying as he'd made her out to be. That couldn't be right, he decided. Aubin was just really, really good at this. The boy obviously possessed an almost supernatural ability to charm the opposite sex. He could get laid every night if he really wanted to. Yeah. That was it.

Lazzy allowed the moment to linger for a few seconds longer before interjecting. "Shall we?"

Samantha released Aubin's hand and shook her head to try to snap herself back to reality. "Lead the way," she said sleepily. Beside her, Hirace looked like he wanted to speak to the manager.

The group fell into step behind Lazzy. Dash strategically took the rear as usual, but this time Keighlan fell back to walk beside him. She pointed at the severe lack of distance between Samantha and Aubin and squeezed Dash's hand.

"What's it like having such famous parents?" the girl asked.

Aubin cocked his head thoughtfully. "It's fun and difficult and rewarding and taxing and a billion other contradictory things all at once," he replied. "I'm just glad I got my mother's good looks."

Samantha actually giggled. "Sounds...complicated. And sort of lonely."

He shrugged. "Well, maybe we can commiserate sometime. Seems like you're not too far from finding out what it's like all on your own. Your father's the Pintiri. That may not mean a lot to you right now, but you'll quickly discover just how important his role is as you learn more about Evitankari and the other magic communities sprinkled across the globe."

"That's what I'm afraid of." They shared another laugh, and Keighlan squeezed Dash's hand again. He still couldn't fathom what he was seeing, but he wasn't going to argue with it.

Their walk was pleasant and relaxing. He and Keighlan had always enjoyed a nice brisk walk at dusk. The weather mages monitoring Evitankari never allowed the temperature to drift too high or too low, but they permitted just enough deviance to make the seasons mean something. That night, however, was unseasonably chilly—but not uncomfortably so. Dash could feel Keighlan sliding contentedly through the heavy air beside him, but he was far too annoyed with his situation to acknowledge or appreciate her company.

The nearest stretch of Evitankari's city wall was a mere three blocks from their meeting point. The blue and black stone structure soon loomed before them. White runes covered its surface like esoteric formulas on some deranged mathematician's chalkboard. Dash recognized a few of them from his schooling, but he'd never understood how they all worked together to create the directional wards that deterred unwanted visitors from coming too close to the city. Some things, he'd long ago decided, weren't worth the time it took to learn them.

Lazzy fell back into step beside Samantha, leaving Gearix to lead the pack. "Fun bit of Lightning Club trivia for you," he said. "Keighlan often used to study at the base of the watchtower around the corner when she wanted privacy to focus on a particularly hard assignment."

Samantha looked at him in confusion. "That wasn't in the books. Keighlan always studied under the tree in her backyard," she insisted. "The city wall is never even mentioned."

"They made that part up!" Lazzy declared, sweeping his arm across his chest like a gameshow host revealing a terrific prize. "Artistic license and all that."

Dash couldn't help himself. "Supposedly it made her seem more approachable and less like a weird loner."

She elbowed him in the ribs. "And you two always thought I didn't see you spying on me from the alleys."

"You saw us?" Dash said incredulously.

"Of course she did," Gearix replied. "You two were always as subtle as a troll trying to rob a bank when it came to your interest in Keighlan."

"Were not," Lazzy said, his face flushed.

"Were too," Gearix teased. "Everybody knew you guys were constantly drooling over her."

"I never drooled," Dash said with exaggerated indignation. The group shared a laugh. For a moment, it felt just like the old days: trekking across Evitankari to investigate a flimsy lead with just a tight group of good friends. He savored the feeling for a few seconds before dismissing it. That way, Dash knew, led to danger.

With a devious twinkle in his eye, Lazzy stepped up to the wall and knocked on it three times. Summoning its frightening guardian in front of people who'd never met the beast had always been one of his favorite pranks. "Ever taken the Path to Port?" he asked Samantha.

"This'll be my first time," she replied. "I'm excited to meet this Ornock guy my father told me about."

Lazzy's shoulders slumped in disappointment. "Yes, well, the old gnoll is certainly a singular individual."

A mechanism inside the wall clicked and a three-foot wide section slid down into the ground, revealing the narrow road beyond—and its gatekeeper, the towering Ornock dia nu li Ulanapai. "Name and purpose?" he rumbled. The intimidating expression on his long, horse-like face suddenly softened. "Oh, the Lightning Club!"

"In the flesh, Big O," Lazzy said with a dramatic bow. "Anything you'd like signed today?"

Ornock's lean muscles flexed beneath his cloak as he reached up to scratch the knobby skin inside the ring of horns atop his head. "There are several things I'd like autographed, but I neglected to bring them to work today." Dash tried to picture the ugly gnoll getting ready in the morning and absolutely could not process the idea.

"We could stop back over tomorrow, if you're on the schedule," Lazzy offered. Dash felt Keighlan stifle a groan. He sympathized.

"I'll be here," Ornock said proudly. He stepped aside to let them pass.

Gearix reached up to pat the big gnoll's shoulder as she and Lazzy strode by. "See you soon, Ornock," she said cheerily. Aubin followed them without acknowledging the beast.

Dash and his wife proceeded next. Keighlan always privately insisted that he keep himself between her and Ornock whenever they went to Port. The gnoll just plain freaked her out—not because of his size or appearance, but simply because he didn't make any sense to her. No one had ever conclusively proven whether Ornock was a real, live gnoll, or a spirit inhabiting the wall, or some manifestation of the ancient runes scratched into the stone, or something else entirely. Keighlan's encyclopedic knowledge of sorcery left her extremely wary of any magic she couldn't explain in detail. Dash had no problem serving as a buffer in this case. He'd always sort of liked Ornock's no-nonsense approach.

The gnoll suddenly shifted to block Samantha and Hirace. "Name and purpose?" he rumbled. The Lightning Club stopped and turned back to watch. Dash hoped Samantha would piss herself and run home to her father. Surely the ugly, imposing beast would finally—finally—make the girl sweat a bit. Surely.

As usual, she didn't even blink. "I'm Samantha Brooks, the Pintiri's daughter and Chief of Staff," she said matter-of-factly. "This is Hirace, medic of the Gadukah and my security detail for the day. We're accompanying the Lightning Club in their investigation."

Ornock didn't respond for several seconds. "I detect a resemblance to Roger Brooks, but you have not been approved to visit Port today and your position does not afford you perpetual travel rights."

Lazzy gave Dash a little elbow in the side. As members of the Combined Council, any of the four of them could've preapproved Samantha's access to Port. Lazzy had offered to take care of the necessary paperwork for both Aubin and Samantha earlier in the day. Obviously he'd decided it would be more fun to mess with the girl a bit.

Samantha leaned around the gnoll to look the Lightning Club's way. "Council of Sorcery Keighlan, would you be so kind?"

The impatience tinging Keighlan's voice betrayed her annoyance with Lazzy's prank. "Of course, my dear. Ornock, Samantha and Hirace are guests of my office today. Please allow them full, unfettered access to Path and to Port, as per my authority."

The gnoll immediately stepped aside. "Acknowledged. Samantha Brooks, Hirace, please remember that although the Council of Sorcery's command grants you immediate access to the facilities I protect, this exception is only temporary and does not exclude you from the base regulations governing the use of these areas."

"We understand," Samantha replied easily. "Thank you for the explanation."

And so they continued on, leaving Ornock alone behind them. Dash thought he could feel real heat rising off his wife's body as she glared lasers into Lazzy's back. He glanced over his shoulder to check on Samantha and Hirace. Neither seemed bothered, but Dash suspected they both knew exactly what had just happened—and that they'd remember it later. Gearix probably wasn't happy either. "Lazzy's definitely going to be sleeping on the couch tonight," he whispered to Keighlan.

Path provided them just barely enough room to proceed in pairs. Dense with runes, the walls on either side of them crackled with magical energy. Accessible at any point of the city wall, Path adjusted itself automatically to accommodate whoever or whatever traveled through it, and it always connected to Port at the far end. Dash had often thought it would've been a lot easier to just put in a bus.

"So I've been wondering about something," Samantha said tentatively. "Helen Mirtz, the author of the Lightning Club series: real person?"

"Helen is very real," Keighlan said quickly, as if to cut off any potential shenanigans. "And she's a total sweetheart."

Dash agreed. There were few people on the planet he thought of as legitimately good, but the woman who'd brought their story to the masses was one of them. They'd met her a few times—in disguise, of course—and she'd always come off as an absolute ray of sunshine who truly believed in and enjoyed her work. All the dust she'd been fed by her handlers to keep her on script probably hadn't hurt in that regard.

"Is she in on...all this?" Samantha continued.

"No," Keighlan replied. "The original publisher of the series is a Tallisker subsidiary. They identified Helen as an ideal fit due to her earlier work in the young adult space and approached her with an offer after we gave our approval. Evitankari often hires contractors through the demons' corporation when it has business interests among humanity."

"The Combined Council negotiated with Tallisker on our behalf," Gearix interjected. "There were several details they deemed too sensitive for publication. They changed the name of our city to Heartsburrow, for instance, and modified the specifics of its security and layout. Much of the way magic works in the books is also very different from how it works in practice."

"The decision to set the series in a post-apocalyptic utopia is particularly interesting in hindsight," Samantha said.

Keighlan giggled. "The Council has always thought very highly of Evitankari's ability to endure."

"Even now?"

"I suppose so," Keighlan said thoughtfully. "Although we often cling desperately to the past, we elves are nothing if not adaptable. We wouldn't have survived this long otherwise."

"Hear, hear!" Lazzy declared in a tone that's been considered douchy since the late nineties rise of the antihero. "We are elves, and we are survivors!" He raised his fist triumphantly, then lowered it when he realized no one else was playing along.

"But the past is the past, and I'm worried about the present," Keighlan said hesitantly. "Evitankari's a powerful player, but the tip-top of Tallisker's leadership structure was just killed in our territory. The demon lord we all assumed dead and gone just popped out of a statue. Sure, your mother and father put him down, but there's going to be fallout, and I don't know if the city's ready for it—militarily, economically, or politically."

Dash winced. Though his wife wasn't wrong—not by a long shot—that last bit hit way too close to home. Surely any threat to Evitankari would flee in terror when it learned he'd spent an afternoon making papier-mâché moo cows with a ten-year-old who could blow snot bubbles the size of bowling balls. When he was done making silly jokes in his head, he realized how much it hurt that Keighlan was just bringing her concerns up now, and in mixed company. Why hadn't she come to him with all of this first? She'd always done so in the past, but she'd also been either sloshed or hung over at the time. Did she not trust him? And if this was some attempt to reach out to the Brooks camp, why hadn't she discussed it with him? Dash loved Keighlan, but the thought of her embracing some sort of newfound agency and independence made him uncomfortable. Sobriety, Dash was coming to realize, was a hell of a drug.

"You're not the only one who's worried," Samantha said. "We're all in a weird spot."

"Tell me about it," Gearix replied. "Aldern left me a pair of shoes I don't feel even remotely qualified to fill. At work, all I hear about is 'the way things used to be.' It's odd to realize that the time they're so obsessed with is a mere week and a half in the past. Elven sorcerers have never been that great at keeping detailed documentation; they hoard their processes and discoveries and only share with others they deem worthy. My predecessor was no exception. We lost so much institutional knowledge when the Witch's bottle giant destroyed the Kralak and wiped out most of the mages that no one really knows how 'the way things used to be' actually worked."

Oh, it's weird for you? Dash thought. *Today I sang a song about shearing sheep and learned how to spell the word "tractor."*

"At least we have each other," Lazzy said. "Nothing can stop us as long as we're together!"

Dash had always simultaneously hated and admired his friend's persistence with sappy bullshit. "We won't be stopping anything if you make us all vomit," he said merrily, sensing an opportunity to deflect a conversation that was making him more and more uncomfortable.

The group laughed. Keighlan stroked his shoulder. "As Council of Medicine, I second my husband's concerns!" she said to an additional round of laughter.

Slipping into funny sidekick mode wasn't as easy as it used to be, but Dash was pleased that he hadn't lost any of his ability to defuse tense situations. He made a mental note to follow up with Keighlan later—in private.

Port's exterior wall appeared abruptly ahead of them two bends later. Evitankari's customs house was a tall but nondescript stone tower. Keighlan used to joke that whenever she looked up at its higher levels she expected to see some long-forgotten princess's golden, flowing locks dangling down the side from a distant window. Lazzy strode purposefully up to the stone and knocked three times. If there was one thing his friend loved more than sappy bullshit, Dash knew, it was operating magic doors. The wall slid down into the ground and they continued inside.

The building's architecture wasted no time getting them to their destination, depositing the group right into Port's cavernous first floor warehouse. As they paused to get their bearings, Samantha stepped ahead to gawk at the towering rows of packed shelves. "My father's stories really didn't do this place justice," she said.

Dash was so relieved that Samantha Brooks was finally impressed by something that he took the lead in elaborating. "Every item and person entering or leaving Evitankari travels through Port. Customs staff examines everything for compliance. There's a transpoint in the very center that connects us to the rest of the world. In a given year, Port typically processes hundreds of billion dollars worth of goods and several thousand travelers." He'd seen more than a few documentaries on the subject.

Samantha watched with interest as a trio of elves sorted a pallet of dog-sized crystals into bins by color. Across the aisle, a young man inserted a stick thermometer into a cardboard box that appeared to be breathing. Behind him, a woman with a clipboard carefully catalogued a shelf packed to bursting with mason jars full of what might've been rainbows.

"It's like a beehive," Samantha said as her eyes darted back and forth, trying to take it all in.

"Coming through!" a burly elf with puffy red cheeks bellowed as he pushed a cart loaded with heavy kegs past her. Samantha stepped aside, but he stopped anyway. "Hey! Aren't you that new Pintiri's daughter?"

Dash swore Lazzy flinched hard enough to generate a breeze. The members of the Lightning Club weren't used to not being immediately recognized and greeted, and playing second fiddle to Samantha Brooks—of all people—was like a slap in the face.

Samantha eyed the man with suspicion for a moment before visibly relaxing. This was new for her too. "I'm also his Chief of Staff," she said tentatively.

"Well, congrats on the promotion!" the worker replied gregari-ously. "Your father did us all a real solid in Old Ev. Love to grab that guy a beer sometime, formally welcome him to the neighbor-hood and all."

One less drink for us, Lazzy's brief scowl complained. Beside him, Gearix found something interesting to study on the floor.

"Dad would love that," Samantha said, "but keep it to one or he might drink your whole paycheck."

The elf's cheeks somehow got even redder as they parted for his big, toothy smile. "My kind of guy! I'm Liyo, by the way."

"Samantha Brooks," she replied as she shook his meaty hand. "Pleased to meet you." She hesitated for a moment, half-turning as if she'd just remembered she wasn't alone. Dash knew what was coming next and he prayed Lazzy's head wouldn't explode. "Have you met my friends, the Lightning Club?"

Liyo leaned forward and squinted at Aubin. "Lazzy, right?"

"That's my son," Lazzy growled. His kid smirked like an asshole, just like Uncle Dash taught him.

"Ah, so it is!" Liyo's beady eyes swept across them all with just the faintest hint of recognition. He ran his hand through his scraggly, thinning hair. "So what are you all doing in Port today?"

"We're here to see Balacath," Keighlan replied.

"My man, Captain Buckets!" Liyo crowed.

"Captain...Buckets?"

"Balacath's in charge of waste management around here. Those big blue buckets you see my compatriots wheeling around and tossing contraband into? Each contains a singularity. A black hole." As if on command, an elf in the nearest aisle hoisted a heavy crate toward the mouth of a much smaller garbage bin. The bin sucked that crate down like a child slurping a noodle.

"That can't be safe," Samantha said.

"It is, thanks to Captain Buckets!" Liyo replied. He pointed to their left. "Grab the nearest elevator. Fifth floor. Take a left when you get off, then he's in the fourth office on the right. Can't miss it."

"Many thanks," Lazzy snapped.

The group got moving again. "Dad likes to hang out at Goody Glover's," Samantha told Liyo as they parted company. He thanked her with a smile and a salute and returned to pushing his cart.

"You know, there's more to do in this city than drown yourself in swill at the pub," Aubin said a few steps later.

"Someone should tell my father," Samantha replied.

"As his Chief of Staff, you would be uniquely positioned to influence his behavior."

"Hmm. If only I knew where to tell him to hang out."

"I could help you. Maybe show you around."

She blushed again. "I just might take you up on that offer."

Ahead of them, Lazzy stumbled over his own feet. Even he couldn't believe his dumbass plan to seduce Samantha Brooks was working.

Dash knew from his documentaries that thirty-six evenly spaced elevator shafts tunneled through Port's exterior wall. That the one they needed to reach Balacath's office was a mere three minutes away was almost too convenient. Path opened into the vast warehouse at seemingly random points each trip. Had it somehow known where they needed to be? Dash wasn't sure. What he did know, however, was that Port's upper floors—primarily offices and archives, but probably also a few more interesting things the people in charge had decided the general public didn't need to know about—were impossible mazes of twisting, seemingly random corridors. Researchers debated whether the manic architecture was an accident or some sort of defense mechanism. Dash suspected it was just due to some asshole having a good time making things more complicated and ridiculous than they needed to be, as often happened in Evitankari. Sometimes he worried his own life fit that description.

A pair of shiny steel doors marked the entrance to their elevator. Lazzy pressed the accompanying button to summon the car, triggering the acknowledgement of an electronic bell and a distant whir of equipment. Palpable awkwardness settled over the group as they watched a little LED screen laboriously count down from fifteen. Dash's mind drifted back to his documentaries, which had never shown anything past the sixth floor. Keycard access kept the riffraff from traveling higher. He realized then that as Council of Agriculture he could probably find out what was up there. Perhaps another day.

Aubin elbowed Samantha playfully. "Ornock's ugly cousin guards this elevator," he said.

"No he doesn't," Hirace snapped. Dash had almost forgotten Samantha's Gadukah watchdog was with them. The young man didn't look pleased.

To her credit, Samantha merely shook her head—but not without the slightest twitch of a smile tugging at the corner of her mouth.

The screen flipped from two to one, the elevator car settled in place with a mechanical groan, and the doors slid open. A couple dozen people would've fit inside. They took up positions around the perimeter, staring crosswise at each other. Keighlan settled heavily against the wall beside Dash, just out of his reach. The set of her jaw and the distant glimmer in her eye meant she was trying to parse something important—and that she was at least a little pissed. Dash hadn't seen her like that since she'd reached the legal drinking age. It made him uncomfortable.

Lazzy punched the button for five. The bell chimed again, the doors squeezed shut, and the car lurched upward. As Dash understood it, an office on the fifth floor meant Balacath was somewhere in the middle of Port's management structure. He probably had a few subordinates, but it was unlikely he was allowed to call too many shots on his own.

"This elevator's electric?" Samantha asked from in between Hirace and Aubin. Her hard eyes begged Keighlan for a rescue.

The other woman obliged. "Yes, although the shafts through which they travel were likely dug out using sorcery. Up until fifty-something years ago, the only access to Port's upper levels was via a steep staircase circling the exterior."

The documentaries hadn't included that bit. Dash scratched his head.

"So why not magic the elevators too?" Samantha asked. "Or the mechanisms controlling them?"

No one offered an immediate answer. Gearix shrugged. "At some point, someone decided technology could do the job just as well for cheaper."

Keighlan changed the subject. "Anyone else a little worried about Balacath and his black holes?"

"A little," Dash admitted.

Lazzy rolled his eyes and took a step away from the wall. "I defeated that slime ball once. I can do it again."

No one felt like arguing, although Dash could tell from the set of Keighlan's jaw that she was considering it. Balacath had always been a sticky subject with her. *A good brainwashing will do that to someone.* The thought made him shiver.

The bell sounded one final time as the elevator lurched to a halt and the doors slid open. Bright fluorescent lights in the adjoining hallway made the white walls and floors seem to glow. As they disembarked, Dash noticed that the corridor wasn't quite as clean as it first seemed. Dirt and dust caked the rubber baseboard like piles of snow plowed to the side of a road. Maintenance hadn't bothered to fill the cracks and pocks in the drywall. A musty aroma tinged the air. It was the perfect space to stash a few unwanted employees. *Exactly where a slug like Balacath belongs,* Dash thought in Lazzy's voice.

"Ready to meet one of the worst villains the Lightning Club has ever encountered?" Aubin asked Samantha.

She clicked her tongue. "I've already met your father's ego, so..."

Aubin burst out laughing. "You're grounded," Lazzy said playfully as the others snickered.

According to the nameplate on the door, Balacath's office was right where Liyo had said it was. The group hesitated; no one wanted to make the first move. As far as Dash knew, none of his friends had seen Balacath since their climactic showdown outside Kron the Withered's lair, although he'd occasionally wondered what had become of their former rival and classmate. In his head, Balacath had degenerated into an ugly, fetid, overweight slob with body odor and acne issues that would keep him from ever finding anything even remotely resembling happiness. He realized almost immediately that he was projecting his worries about his own fate and banished the image entirely.

Something in Balacath's office shrieked angrily. Dash flinched against the sound, which he could only describe as like a refrigerator being dropped into a wood chipper. The scream ended as abruptly as it began, and it was followed by a familiar and oddly relieving "Aww, fish sticks!"

Lazzy rapped his knuckles against the door. "Balacath? Everything okay in there?"

The ensuing silence spoke volumes. Dash pictured Balacath scrambling to hide his vast collection of empty potato chip bags and microwave dinner trays, then attempting to organize his myriad fleshy folds into a vaguely elven and barely presentable shape, all while spritzing the air with various canned fragrances that didn't stand a chance against the overpowering musk radiating from every surface in his disgusting lair.

"I'm okay!" Balacath replied almost a full minute later. "It's okay. Is...is Gearix with you?"

She and Lazzy traded a glance Dash couldn't parse. "I'm here," she said warmly.

"Okay. Good."

A few more seconds passed. Obviously Balacath had discovered a couple more pizza boxes that needed to be stashed somewhere. The lock clicked and the door gently popped open. Dash prepared himself to gag at the overpowering stench that would soon waft out and consume them all, but it never came. Lazzy eased the door open a little further and waved his wife inside. The others quickly followed. Hirace made a point of entering before Samantha, which she obviously didn't like but also didn't argue with. Dash stepped inside last and shut the door behind himself. Privacy was warranted here, but he kept his hand on the knob—just in case.

Much to Dash's surprise and chagrin, Balacath's office wasn't a steaming pile of garbage and misery. It was clean, orderly, and pleasantly cozy. Bookshelves lined the walls, packed tightly with alphabetized tomes and a few nautical knick-knacks. Aubin plopped himself onto a stately leather couch to the group's left and sank deep into the cushions. Balacath's desk was a wide wooden beast topped with a simple lamp, a closed laptop, and a few small stacks of manila folders stuffed with documents. The place even smelled sort of nice, thanks to a small brazier of incense smoking in the corner.

Balacath looked sharp in his pressed khakis and blue shirt and tie. He'd kept the ragged white skunk stripe that had been singed into his dark hair during his battle with Lazzy outside Kron the Withered's lair. There was no sign of skin problems or oppressive body odor. In fact, Balacath had grown into a reasonably handsome man. Dash grasped for solace in the fact that Captain Buckets was still a spindly runt with useless stick arms.

"I'm at a complete loss," Balacath said to Gearix. The excited twinkle in his icy blue eyes matched the energy of his fluttering hands. "I've never seen Judy in such a state."

Gearix gingerly lifted the lid of the big blue trash barrel they were discussing and peered inside. "These things are a little outside my experience," she said hesitantly.

Balacath's hands kicked into high gear. "It's just a smidge of exotic matter kept in local context using a Parsthen concentrate backed with an inverse sprill hex. Don't let the strangeness of the subject fool you; it's just a clever use of the concepts we learned in third-year dynamic electromancy."

Dash knew they'd all taken that class, but his only memory of it was Professor Thern's hyperactive Adam's apple. *Try keeping that thing in local context with a spell, hotshots!* he thought.

"A sprill, huh?" Gearix shut the lid and leaned back. "And you said it's producing abnormal harmonic resonance?"

"Yes," Balacath replied. "Judy emits an ear-piercing shriek every fifty-seven minutes—like the one you heard when you arrived. The warehouse staff finds it worrisome."

"A black hole that screams," Lazzy muttered. "Why would anyone worry about that?"

"Oh!" Gearix interjected. "The hex's boundary must be frayed..."

Balacath nodded in agreement. "...destabilizing the lattice of the concentrate, leading to a pressure buildup and regularly timed expulsion, yes. But what caused it? And why does the problem keep returning? I've patched that boundary three times now."

"What's it been...eating...lately?"

"Same old. Judy's been on textile and paper duty for the last six years."

"Sounds dull," Lazzy quipped.

"Change in routine?" Gearix asked, ignoring her husband. "Different maintenance schedule?"

"None."

"Staffing?"

"Now that you mention it, yes. The shrieking began around the same time a new journeyman inspector started in Judy's division." He paused. "Foul play seems unlikely."

"Maybe it's negligence rather than malice." Gearix tapped her foot. "What do you know about the new guy?"

"Girl. Not much. High marks in the academy, friendly and personable. Sometimes the others complain about her lunch. She microwaves fish once a week."

Gearix's eyes lit up. "...releasing a regular burst of unstable antineutrinos..."

"...that perforate the sprill's boundary and throw the whole system out of whack! Gearix, you're still a genius!"

They high-fived merrily as the others looked on in confusion. The moment passed quickly and Gearix took a step back, trying to hide her embarrassment.

Balacath sensed the air in the room and wasted no time addressing it. "So. I don't imagine you all stopped in just to say hello."

Lazzy took a deep breath in preparation to unleash some overwrought spiel, but Samantha cut him off. "We've reason to believe Kron the Withered has returned. Know anything about that?" Dash considered cracking the door open to vent the heat streaming from Lazzy's ears. No doubt he'd been up all night, practicing his preferred line of questioning in the mirror.

Their target shifted uncomfortably. "Before I answer...who are you?"

"Samantha Brooks. I'm the Pintiri's Chief of Staff. I represent his office as liaison to the Lightning Club."

"Thank you. That's not exactly a standard assignment for such a position, but we live in strange times. It's a pleasure to meet you, Ms. Brooks, and I hope you'll pass my best wishes on to your father." They exchanged polite nods, and then Balacath paused to gather himself.

The others stopped breathing. Dash felt his spine turn to steel. A quick spark of spell power crackled along Lazzy's left wrist, just in case he needed it. Keighlan looked ready to pounce. Here it was, then: their old rival, brought not quite so low as they thought, kicking his mental machinery into overdrive so as best to screw them over once more. Dash's gaze flicked around the room, from the books on the walls to the rug on the floor to the lamp on the desk to the black hole in the barrel, and he was waylaid by the sudden, sinking feeling that confronting Captain Buckets on his own turf may have been a colossal mistake.

Balacath exhaled. Dash couldn't recall ever having seen him look so ashamed. "I don't think Judy's problem is the fish."

No one knew exactly how to react to that. Lazzy actually quivered, apparently unsure whether to unleash his spell or await further information. Gearix stared at the ceiling as she tried to figure out where she'd gone wrong in her diagnosis. Even Samantha, Aubin, and Hirace appeared perplexed. Dash had no clue what to make of it, so he looked to his wife.

"It's on the barrel, isn't it?" Keighlan asked.

Balacath blushed. "I first noticed it the other day. Also...it's good to see you."

Her face darkened. "Show us. Now."

He gripped Judy's handle with both hands and slowly lowered the barrel to the floor. On the container's bottom, between the wheels, the exact same rune from the morgue and the chalkboard had been carved into the thick blue plastic.

"I thought someone was playing a trick on me," Balacath whispered. "Especially since Judy's not the only one."

"Not the only one?" Lazzy shouted louder than he needed to. The release of all his built-up tension crashed through the room like a wave.

"Judy's the only waste disposal unit emitting the unusual harmonic resonance, so I thought it was unrelated. The staff here's an interesting bunch. There's a lot of practical jokes, and being on the receiving end of one means they accept you, like you're part of the family. I thought—"

"You said there are more," Keighlan growled.

Balacath's cheeks somehow turned even redder. "Yeah. By the way, I don't think I ever ap—"

"How many more?" Samantha demanded.

That snapped Balacath back to reality. He counted on his fingers as he spoke. "Ralph, Constance, Timothy, James, Rose, Willard, Cynthia, Theresa, Peg..." He stopped to consider the count. "I'd need three or four more hands."

Nobody knew what to say. The Lightning Club and their companions hadn't been prepared for a contrite, seemingly innocent Balacath. Samantha in particular looked like she wanted to crawl under a rock. The fangirl had been looking forward to a confrontation just as much as the rest of them, if not more so. When it hadn't materialized, well...there went the fairytale, and all that remained was real life. Dash knew the feeling. It sucked.

Hirace cleared his throat. "I can arrest him."

Although the Gadukah reported only to the Pintiri, Samantha was technically in charge in this case—and she was looking at Keighlan.

Which likely meant this wasn't going to end well for Captain Buckets. Keighlan had never forgiven him for the suggestive hex he'd placed on her after she'd turned down his first invitation to the spring formal. The spell worked far too well, and Keighlan had temporarily fallen head over heels in love with Balacath and begged him to take her to the dance. What was supposed to be one of the happiest moments of a young elven girl's life had instead been turned into a nightmare. Luckily Lazzy and Gearix had managed to break the spell before things had gone too far, but that was a few days and a major life milestone Keighlan would never get back.

The various horrific fates Balacath deserved were a popular topic in Keighlan's late-night drunken rants. If she had her way, he'd be a destitute, one-legged, syphilitic toilet scrubber with no eyebrows, no tastebuds capable of detecting sweetness, and no one willing to attend his birthday parties. Dash thought she was probably going a little too far.

"You should be thrown into the dankest, darkest, most wretched cell in Evitankari and left to wither away," Keighlan said matter-of-factly. "When I was first named the interim Council of Medicine, I seriously considered using my new position to have you locked the fuck up. I will never understand why Aldern pardoned you. Unfortunately for us...we need your help."

Balacath wobbled in confusion. "You...you do?"

"We do?" Lazzy asked, just as lost.

"We do. It's obvious Kron the Withered is trying to make contact. When he does, we need to know—and then we'll have him."

Balacath considered that for a few seconds. "Alright. It's the least I can do. But what if it's not me he wants? What if it's something here in Port?"

"Then you're well-positioned to identify that too. But make no mistake: I'm going to have the Council of Intelligence place you under twenty-four-hour surveillance until we find Kron. Everything you do will be documented. And if you so much as take a piss I don't like, I've got a dungeon with your name on it."

— CHAPTER THIRTEEN —

Samantha glanced side to side at the chunky old warehouses lining the road and sighed. "This isn't the way we came, so it's probably not the way back home."

"You're right," Hirace replied.

"Elaborate, please."

"You told Aubin you'd like to be introduced to some fun things to do in Evitankari. I figured I'd help you do that so you don't have to subject yourself to that douchebag."

The last thing Sam needed was a bodyguard jealous of her feigned interest in a boy who was obviously just stringing her along at his father's behest. She was sort of offended that Hirace seemed to think she was dumb enough to fall for Aubin's act. Maybe she'd played the part of the naïve, starstruck girl too well. "I'm not actually into Aubin, you know."

"Oh, I know," he replied just awkwardly enough to imply he didn't believe it. "I'm worried that you're not actually into *Evitankari*. This place is likely to be your home for a while. You should get to know the city and its people better, try to find a few things about it you enjoy."

That wasn't the worst idea. Sam knew she couldn't spend her entire life hiding inside her wonderful new home, reading reports and studying history and daydreaming about a return to the human world. Her job as Chief of Staff had gotten her out and about quite often, but those experiences were all colored through the lens of work. She needed places to hang out, things to do, and friends to spend time with. Hirace could help with all that. Although Sam didn't particularly enjoy his company and she was worried about leading him on, at least she knew she could trust him.

At that moment, however, there was a rather large reason to ask for a raincheck. "I really, really need to talk to Driff about Balacath," she said.

Hirace's eyes flicked upward for a moment. The Gadukah didn't need to do anything other than think to access the telepathic network linking them all together, but each of them had a little tic they deployed when they wanted others around them to know they were using it. "Commander Rynes will contact the Council of Intelligence and ask him to meet us at our destination."

"Fine. Where are we going?"

"To the Scar."

"Capital S?"

"It is important enough to our history that it's become a proper noun, yes."

The cobblestones ended, replaced by a well-worn dirt path winding up into a row of brown, barren hills. Here and there hearty tufts of defiant grass popped up from the hard ground. A few bent, skeletal trees shorter than Samantha clung desperately to life like men on the brink of dehydration.

"This doesn't look like the direction to fun," Sam said.

Hirace nodded. "Trust me, it's out there. The organizers like the juxtaposition. When Axzar was defeated by the first Pintiri, the vast majority of his demon horde fled—save for a few thousand under the command of the Devourer's most brutal general,

Prytoris. That host spent six months harassing Evitankari from a camp in what became the Scar before they were finally rooted out."

"And the land never recovered," Sam added sarcastically. "Right?"

"Basically. We've got magic that can make tomatoes grow on a beach, but no one's ever figured out how to fix the soil here." He paused. "Some researchers think the magic used to destroy Prytoris and his followers is just as much to blame as the demons themselves."

"Does everything around here possess some dark secret, or are your people just genetically paranoid?"

Hirace chuckled. "In my experience, it's a little of both. There were all sorts of wild rumors and legends about the statue in Tash Square before a long-dead demon lord popped out of it."

They crested the initial rise, which turned out to be much steeper on the other side. Their pace slowed as they gingerly shuffled down into a narrow gulley that may have once been a riverbed. Another small hill awaited them a hundred paces further along.

"Is that music?" Sam asked.

"Bluegrass," Hirace replied. "Lubby and the Panhandlers are playing the Scar tonight."

That was the exact moment Sam knew for sure her father had put Hirace up to this. Roger had been trying to get her into bluegrass for years. He'd taken her to her first show when she was five, and the genre had been a constant presence on road trips, at barbecues, and on lazy Sunday afternoons on the back porch. She'd hated it at first, but it sort of grew on her as she aged, to the point where she'd been to a few small shows on her own in the last couple of years. Something in her chest warmed. If it would make her father happy, she could spend an hour or two with Hirace.

"Hold on," she said when they reached the bottom of the hill. The loose dirt in the gulley puffed up in little clouds of dust with every step they took. "You elves turned a ruined battlefield into a live music venue?"

"That we did," Hirace replied with a proud smile. "Prytoris's incursion was a serious wound to Evitankari. We decided the best way to memorialize it was to literally dance on his grave."

"You guys are weird."

"Hmm. Most of us would argue that 'weird' would entail building a solemn monument no one ever visits instead. Evitankari never wastes something that might someday be useful."

"So I've heard."

They started up the next hill. Sam soon cursed her heavy breathing, more so when she realized Hirace hadn't even broken a sweat. In a town where everyone went everywhere by foot and cars were looked at as filthy and unnecessary, poor conditioning wouldn't be a problem for very long.

"What do you think of the Lightning Club?" she asked, hoping that making Hirace talk at length would at least leave him slightly winded.

"They're about what I expected," he answered quickly. "You?"

That hadn't gone the way she'd planned. "How so?"

"All those former hero types are the same: beaten down, frustrated, lacking a clear path with no clue how to find one, surprised that life's challenges continue on after their big victory, and incapable of understanding why their past success doesn't mean they're immediately handed everything they want."

"And that's typical?"

"Textbook. The problem with saving the world—or even just a small part of it—is that the world continues. What seems at first to be a happy ending is just another chapter in the story. Your victory's sweet, but it doesn't last. You still have to get up the next morning and deal with a whole host of new problems, many of which seem insignificant compared to what you just faced. You've fought and scraped and sacrificed to achieve what felt like the ultimate be-all, end-all goal, but life's still not perfect—and you have to vacuum the rug in the hallway, and make sure the kids get to school, and find a way to deal with the lingering effects and stresses of fighting for everyone's safety. And then, because the weird group of circumstances that positioned you to be a hero in the first place are extremely unlikely to repeat themselves, another big problem comes along, and another group of warriors valiantly faces it down, and you're yesterday's news. So yeah. The Lightning Club isn't the first, and they sure won't be the last. It's a cycle that's been steadily whirling around since we founded this city."

"That's bleak."

"Maybe. Or maybe it's hopeful. No matter the problems we need to solve, there's always someone new ready to step up and make sure the job gets done."

The sharp crescendo of a fiddle solo greeted them at the top of the next hill. Sam was relieved to find a set of deep, blocky stairs carved into the ensuing slope. Below, a crooked crater took a giant bite out of the base of the next hill, forming a jagged cavern that now served as the Scar's main stage. There, a five-piece band played an energetic tune Samantha recognized but couldn't name. There were a few elves seated on the stairs, but most of those in attendance were dancing across the valley floor, weaving around the bright flames of small campfires.

She liked it immediately.

"Come on," Hirace said with a friendly smile. "We'll sit and wait for Driff."

They found a spot on the stairs a quarter of the way down, far from the rest of the crowd. Sam sat with her back to the step behind them, stretching her legs out straight. Hirace took a seat by her left shoulder, just close enough to be heard over the music.

The lead guitarist sang into an old metal microphone dangling from the ceiling of the cavern, but there wasn't any other technology in sight. "Where are the speakers?" Sam asked.

"They're hidden in and around the cavern," Hirace explained. "Turns out the Scar's acoustics make it function as a natural amplifier. Like it?"

"Better than a monument no one ever visits."

It was much, much better than that, but she wasn't quite ready to admit that to Hirace. She didn't want to encourage him, lest he become overconfident and ask her to dance. Instead, she closed her eyes and focused on the music. She didn't need to see the band to enjoy them, didn't need to watch the enthusiastic crowd to know everyone around her was having a good time. There was an energy in that space unlike anything she'd felt elsewhere in Evitankari. Whereas the rest of the city seemed tense and taut like a spring, the Scar radiated peace and contentedness. Sam's heart rate and breathing slowed. Muscles she hadn't realized were tense and twisted finally loosened. Best of all, Hirace kept his big mouth politely shut. She relaxed in a way she hadn't managed to in weeks.

The band chugged through three more songs before a familiar presence darkened the air. She kept her eyes shut for a few additional seconds before giving in to duty. "Did your people plant Kron the Withered's rune on the garbage bins in Port?"

Driff pushed his spectacles up on his nose. "No. We assumed leaving it in the morgue would be more than enough to keep the Lightning Club busy."

"Shit."

Sam quickly recounted their visit with Balacath. The Council of Intelligence listened placidly, but something about his bearing suggested he was not happy. Hirace kept a careful watch on the crowd, just in case any of the elves in attendance became too inquisitive. None ventured close enough to eavesdrop.

When she finished, Driff withdrew a manila folder from somewhere in the depths of his trench coat. "One of my researchers found something interesting in the archives while investigating our chief suspect. Look at this."

The folder contained a small stack of photographs atop a pile of ratty old documents. "That's the director of the morgue," Sam said, examining the first.

"Cark. Accepting a plaque thanking him for twenty-five years of service."

She flipped to the next photo, which was faded and creased and featured an elf who looked far too proud of his bright orange gelatin mold packed tight with fruit. "Same guy. He hasn't aged a bit. Does he still have terrible taste in desserts?"

"Kark with a K, according to the accompanying notes in the archives. And yes—we found the offending pan in the cabinet beside his stove."

"And this black-and-white one is him in a Model T."

"Carrk with a C and two Rs. That's the first automobile ever brought to Evitankari."

"And this...wow, this one's ancient. I'm guessing this isn't one of those old-timey photos you can get at the county fair. He looks like an octogenarian here, though." Still, the tingle running up and down her spine told Sam that was definitely the elf from the other two images. Hirace leaned close to get a look for himself over her shoulder.

"Caark, with two As," Driff said. "Supposedly just a share-cropper in that one."

Gripped with curiosity and something akin to fear, Sam rifled through the old documents. "His death certificate. A birth certificate for Carrk. A bill of sale for three of Kaarc's breeding rams. The deed to Carkk's home. Driff, what the heck? Have you shown my father?"

"I have. He initially thought I was playing a trick on him."

"You blame him?"

"Not really, no."

"Have you brought this Cark guy in?" Hirace asked.

Driff shook his head. "We can't find him. The man's disappeared."

Samantha shut the folder and handed it back to the Council of Intelligence. "Driff, seriously—what's going on?"

He stashed the folder back in his coat and leaned back to watch the band. "I have a theory. Ever hear of a little town in Illinois called Harksburg?"

— CHAPTER FOURTEEN —

Cleaning the chalkboard was one of Dash's least favorite tasks. It reminded him far too much of the day he'd first found Kron the Withered's rune. The professor whose name he couldn't remember had caught him doing something shitty he couldn't remember to Gearix and sentenced him to detention, which meant a heaping helping of "quiet study" and a turn cleaning the blackboard and all of the accompanying accessories. When he'd first swiped an eraser across the strange rune in the corner and it returned almost immediately, he thought he was seeing things. When he tried again and it still wouldn't fade, he knew something strange was going on.

And so it was with great trepidation that Dash erased Nitch's crooked, overly fluffy attempt to draw an absolute unit of a sheep. To his profound relief, the impossible creature did not return to the slate. Dash thought it had looked more like a buffalo anyway, despite Lesryn's positive reinforcement. There was no way a real sheep could ever grow that big, elven agricultural magic or not.

He took a step back and examined the misspelled vegetable names covering the remainder of the board, the rows of empty desks behind him, and then the dusty concrete at his feet, which he was supposed to sweep when he'd finished erasing the day's work.

A sudden rage boiled up into his chest, hot and insistent. Maybe he'd finally reached his breaking point. Maybe his worries about Aldern's missing head, Keighlan's independence, and Balacath's general presence had ruined what was left of his patience. Maybe having been unable to sleep the night before because his frazzled brain had insisted on repeatedly evaluating each and every one of the approximately eight thousand ways recent events could ruin the life he'd built with his beautiful wife had left him desperate to at least try to take control. He didn't know, and he didn't really care, and he decided it didn't actually matter.

Lesryn's office was behind a movable partition, in an old stall or pen or whatever. Her lessons hadn't covered it. She looked up placidly as Dash barged in, almost as if she'd been expecting him. "Time to talk, then?" she asked cheerily.

Dash's voice momentarily caught in his throat. "Past time," he growled.

"Alright," she said, nodding to her left. "Let's go out back."

The disgruntled interim Council of Agriculture turned on his heel and stomped toward the rear of the barn. Lesryn's chair scraped across the concrete floor as she rose to join him. Dash knew it was petty and stupid, but leading her outside made him feel as if the pecking order had finally been corrected. He was in charge here, Rot damn it, and Lesryn served at his pleasure. Her job was to prepare him for his new role, not to inundate him with a never-ending deluge of childish bullshit. Confidence buoyed his steps. Boy, was he going to let her absolutely have it when they got outside!

Dash burst out into the daylight with what he'd hoped would be enough raw, angry force to knock the door off its hinges. It wasn't, and the endless rows of corn behind the barn were not impressed. Lesryn stepped outside behind him, wearing the same warm smile she'd greeted him with the day they'd met. He'd been charmed by that smile at first, but now he saw it for exactly what it was: condescending and duplicitous, a snide disguise hiding a true villain masquerading as one of the good guys. He couldn't wait to wipe it off her face.

"Here we are!" Lesryn chirped happily. "Are you going to get in the barrel, or do we have to do this the hard way?"

For a few heartbeats Dash couldn't process Lesryn's words, as if she'd spoken in a different language he'd never learned. Then he noticed the familiar blue garbage barrel parked beside the barn's back door, which he'd stormed right past in his rush to force a confrontation. His breath caught in his throat—and his fucked up tenure as Council of Agriculture suddenly made a lot more sense.

He was pretty sure he could take Lesryn one-on-one in a physical fight, but he had no means of determining what sort of magic she could wield. His own offensive spellcasting had never been great to begin with and he was badly out of practice. Flight would have to take precedence over fight, then. Running through a cornfield seemed dicey, but maybe he could use the barn itself as cover if he could make it around the corner.

Heavy footsteps drew his attention to the left. Corken stepped around the edge of the barn, once again chewing on a stalk of grass. The old man greeted Dash with a wink, then nodded toward the other corner. Dash turned to find the biggest bull he'd ever seen guarding that exit. Nitch's overly muscular interpretation of a sheep had nothing on that huge bastard.

"You can outrun me," Corken drawled. "You can probably outrun Lesryn. No one outruns ol' Jasper over there." He punctuated that last statement by spitting into the dirt at Dash's feet.

Lesryn pushed Balacath's barrel forward and swung the lid open. "It won't kill you," she said. "It's just a little...unpleasant."

"Sort of like your lectures," Dash snapped.

She shrugged. "Agriculture's never been my best subject. Now stop stalling. Jasper's not known for his patience."

The big bull pawed the dirt and snorted.

What remained of Dash's earlier adrenaline surge wouldn't allow him to give in. A plan began to form in his head. "I'm the interim Council of Agriculture," he said smoothly, spreading his hands and taking a few steps toward Lesryn. "I can promote the two of you into any position you want. Maybe something with a convoluted title that doesn't require you to leave the couch more than once or twice a week? Maybe a posting somewhere with a nice view and easy access to a warm swimming hole? I can put Jasper over there out to stud with the prettiest cows."

"We already have everything we could ever want," Corken replied with an evil smile, "and Jasper's got no equipment."

"And neither will you if you don't get this over with," Lesryn said happily. "Get in the—"

Dash snatched her wrist and jerked her toward his chest, hoping to wrap her in a chokehold with which he could force the others to back off. She was only off-balance momentarily. With surprising strength and speed, Lesryn spun her hip into Dash's thigh and elbowed him right in the throat. He went down in a heap, gasping for air. Tears streamed down his face as Jasper mooed in approval.

"Told you he wouldn't go easy," Corken said.

"Help me get this barrel over him, please," Lesryn replied, as if asking one of her students to read the next few paragraphs in the day's lesson.

"Yes ma'am."

They each took hold of one side of Balacath's barrel and hoisted it up off the ground. Dash gasped, spat, and sputtered as they flipped the plastic bin upside down and angled its gaping maw toward him. The singularity inside hid in a thick curtain of darkness from which light couldn't escape. Dash lacked the breath to flee or scream or even beg, so he gargled angrily toward Lesryn's approaching boots. Despite her reassurances, he didn't believe for a second that this wasn't going to be the end of him. Even if they weren't explicitly trying to murder him, he'd seen enough complicated elven magic to know it didn't always function exactly as intended.

His thoughts turned to Keighlan. She'd miss him, right? Even though she'd stopped relying on him for everything? Even if she somehow found out the truth?

Entering the singularity, Dash would later realize, was surprisingly quick and painless. One moment he was there, a cognitive and functional being, and then he simply wasn't. It was like someone had flipped a switch and turned him off. Dash was gone, his component atoms torn asunder by the pocket of impossibly dense matter inside that simple blue barrel.

Being put back together, however, royally fucking sucked. Dash snapped back into being just in time to realize he was falling, although he lacked the awareness and motor function necessary to do anything about it. He landed head- and shoulder-first on what turned out to be an old foam mattress dressed in dinosaur sheets. The pain of the landing paled in comparison to the utter anguish streaming through his suddenly reconstituted neurons. Everything was on fire, and every part of his nervous system screamed for his attention all at once. He rolled onto his back and spasmed, searching desperately for something solid to latch himself onto so he could right the ship.

Dash registered a pair of voices but couldn't parse their words. His senses flickered on and off as his mind struggled to orient itself. A humanoid shape appeared above him, warm and fleshy and oddly bright against the lightless backdrop. He briefly caught the scent of lilac perfume. Something touched his wildly throbbing carotid. Satisfied sounds were exchanged.

In the spaces in between bursts of sensation, his mind pinballed back and forth off the memories that asserted themselves in his flailing consciousness. He relived the sheer joy of being pushed on a swing as a toddler. He watched from the side of the ballroom as teenaged Keighlan, bug-eyed and brainwashed and yet somehow still radiant in a purple gown, slow danced with Balacath. Then he was younger, and proving to a skeptical professor that he could indeed perform magic on his own by teasing a small plant with a tiny burst of static electricity. He bonded with Lazzy all over again thanks to their shared love of chocolate milk. Headmaster Aldern loomed over the Lightning Club, clucking and shaking his head as he mumbled to himself about just what in the world he was going to do with such nosy children.

"Rot, we can't wait for him all day," a friendly voice said, cutting through the din. Dash couldn't place it, despite its familiarity. All he knew for sure was that he'd hoped he'd never have to hear that particular tone ever again—and that hearing it in the first place should've been downright impossible, because its owner was dead.

Recognition dawned. *Oh,* he thought. *Oh fuck.*

Warm energy flowed into his body through the pair of fingers tracking his pulse. His cells lapped it up hungrily, calming themselves when they were satiated. Dash's senses snapped into focus and the world around him became clear.

A middle-aged woman with long copper hair removed her fingers from his neck and smiled at him. Dash knew her but couldn't quite place her, some long-forgotten celebrity whose name waited just beyond the tip of his tongue. "He's awake," she said gently.

"Good, good," said the familiar voice as its owner appeared by her side. "We really need to find a way to ease that transition."

That calculating gaze had haunted Dash's dreams for almost two decades. Aldern. One of Evitankari's most powerful mages. Don't ask about his poundcake unless you've got a few hours to spare. Last time Dash had seen the old elf he'd been pushing three-hundred years old, but somehow the version in front of him appeared to be barely older than fifty. He'd trimmed his formerly voluminous beard into a tight black goatee and flecks of gray colored the hair by his temples. Without all the wrinkles and liver spots, he was a downright handsome man despite his blunt features.

"Dash!" Aldern crowed. "So good to see you! Don't let my youth and obvious virility fool you! 'Tis I, Headmaster Aldern! Well, former Headmaster Aldern. I was Council of Sorcery when that damnable traitor, Aeric, shot me. This is the sort of unnecessary drama that comes when people have inconvenient memories restored."

The implied threat wasn't lost on Dash. "Yes, Headmaster."

"Oh, none of that formality! I believe I'm operating sans title these days."

"You are indeed," the woman replied. Chyve. Renowned medic who saved an estimated two hundred lives over the course of her career. Horrible tipper. "Technically we are both on sabbatical until our next assignments."

"What'd we draw this time?"

"I'm an analyst in Intelligence. You get to be a low-level grunt in the military."

"Wonderful! I really do enjoy learning the latest and greatest in mass murder!"

"Would you like to trade?"

"No. Driff's an asshole."

"I know. You should probably relocate our guest. His fine motor control should return in a few minutes, but in the meantime..."

"Indeed! Can't have those fools in Port dropping an illegal sofa or an unlicensed shipment of chemicals on poor Dash's head!"

Though his mind screamed at his body to roll, wiggle, or shimmy out from underneath the singularity, his muscles refused to respond. Visions of being crushed by a junked refrigerator or perforated by a discarded shipment of knives turned his blood to ice.

An unseen force gripped Dash's shoulders and yanked him up off the mattress. Aldern's fingers glowed green with power as his spell lifted Dash, spun him upright, and maneuvered him toward a living area by the far wall. A pair of mismatched recliners, one blue and plush and the other gray and narrow and occupied by a beady-eyed elf, waited for him among a trio of crates set up as tables. One was decorated with a plastic flamingo lamp and a trio of what appeared to be posable gnome skeletons. Rows of multi-colored Christmas lights twinkled along the wall. As he got closer, Dash realized the ugly rug beneath it all was actually a collection of green-and-white welcome mats laid out side by side to cover the floor. They were in some sort of cave, a squat, round cavern packed with bric-a-brac, rubbish, and various pieces of contraband the Port workers had discarded via Balacath's buckets. There was crap everywhere, some cluttering the floor, some pinned to the walls, some stacked in odd totem shapes that almost reached the ceiling. It reminded Dash of images he'd seen of human garbage dumps, or maybe that silly steakhouse chain he and Keighlan had visited during their trip to Florida.

The elf in the gray recliner leaned forward and greeted Dash with an awkward wave. "Mystery solved?" Cark asked.

"How?" Dash croaked as he was gently deposited into the other chair.

Cark demurred. "Aldern, your answer to that question is always better than mine."

The other elf tapped his chin in thought as he approached. "That one-word question could refer to so many things, though."

"Let's step through them. How'd Dash get here?"

"Our asset on the inside—a nice young lady with terrible taste in lunch—rerouted several of Port's singularities to deposit matter here to our little lair. Quantum point-to-point transmission is untraceable, unlike the transpoint network. We've got bugs in it that can report back on any and all travel, and we're not foolish enough to believe we're the only ones. Fun fact: those barrel-based singularities are typically directed to a matching cousin above the

Pacific Ocean. That island of garbage so many human environmentalists are up in arms about? Our fault!"

Dash's eyes darted back and forth between the two in confusion. His muscles had begun to tingle, and he felt something resembling control beginning to return.

Cark continued. "And how are you and Chyve not just alive, but younger and looking positively dashing?"

Aldern smiled ear to ear, clearly enjoying the show they were putting on. "Death knows not to bite the hands of its masters, shall we?"

"Ooooh, that's a good one. Brand new?"

"Never used before. I'm quite proud of it. To elaborate upon our youth, let's just say we've gotten quite good at putting ourselves back together. There's a fair amount of excess energy generated by the process that a skilled practitioner can harness in some very interesting ways."

"Excellent! Now, onto the most important question: exactly how fucked is Dash?"

"Not at all, if he plays along! If he doesn't..." After pausing for dramatic effect, Aldern's voice turned ice cold. "I've always wondered how his wife would react if I told her the real story of the Lightning Club."

"Okay," Dash croaked, having nothing else.

"Time to move from how to what," Cark said. "As in, what does he have to do to keep his miserable sham of a life intact?"

"This was going to be Balacath's job, but he's being watched far too closely to effectively be blackmailed. Want to fill in for him?"

Dash nodded meekly. Cutting another ominous deal with the insane Headmaster made him feel like a scared teenager all over again.

Aldern leaned in so close their noses almost touched. "Bring me the Brooks children."

— CHAPTER FIFTEEN —

Pressed into a rather uncomfortable VIP booth on a raised platform that ran the length of the cavernous old industrial building's exterior wall, Samantha Brooks looked around the crowded club and wondered for the eighteenth time in the last hour just what the fuck she'd done to deserve this. Hundreds of young elves, many of them wearing next to nothing, bobbed and gyrated across the dance floor and each other in uneven time with an impossibly loud synth-pop soundtrack underneath enough spotlights, lasers, and flashing strobes to make an optometrist weep. A few dozen elves, mostly women, danced alone atop thin metal plates called saucers, suspended twenty feet above the festivities by a crew of mages well-trained in the telekinetic arts. The carefully organized bottles of liquor arranged upon the tiered shelves behind the bar on the far wall reminded Sam of the towering pipes of a church organ, except backlit by a cacophony of colors that made the whole thing look like it was made of stained glass. Female servers in gauzy dresses flittered behind the bar in a desperate attempt to satiate the demanding crowd.

Cynosure, the place was called. According to Aubin, this was one of the former Pintiri's most profitable business ventures. Sam couldn't decide if Rotreego was a smart investor, some kind of dick, or a combination of the two. *If Willowglen is Evitankari's heart,* she thought, *Cynosure is beyond a doubt its asshole.*

"...and that's when I lit his pants on fire and told him to go fuck his sister!" Ivree declared to a round of raucous laughter. Sam couldn't figure out how the Gadukah made her voice carry over the din, but she was damn glad it did—and that the elf had decided to distract Aubin and his meathead cronies by holding court with her seemingly endless supply of weird and obscene stories.

She worked her gaze around the table. Ivree was seated directly across from her, looking at least five years too young for the giant martini in her hand thanks to a pair of pigtails and a red and white babydoll dress. To Sam's right, Aubin continued nursing a blue beer he claimed was more powerful and generated a better buzz than any top shelf liquor. Sam thought it looked like antifreeze.

And then there were Aubin's friends, a trio of stereotypically tall, fit, square-jawed jocks with crewcuts, slack-jawed expressions, and blank stares. Supposedly they were three quarters of the starting infield for one of the local baseball teams. Sam couldn't tell them apart or remember any of their names, but she didn't like the way the one with the piercing blue eyes kept looking at her. An intense intelligence briefly broke through his otherwise dull façade whenever his attention drifted her way. She couldn't tell if he meant her harm or if there was an actual brain somewhere in his thick skull that had identified her as a kindred spirit in that sea of douchebaggery. She supposed it didn't matter, because she knew better than to trust him either way.

Sam took a quick sip of her painkiller, forced a smile, and tried to relax. The coconut-y drink was delicious, but her limited experience with alcohol made her wary of the comforting warmth that followed. This wasn't exactly what she'd pictured when she'd agreed with Driff and her father to be the bait. Had she known she was going to have to spend an evening in a loud, sweaty, expensive club in a tight black cocktail dress, entertaining a bunch of meatheads with an insane elven sorceress, she would have at least considered saying no. At least she looked fantastic. The insane elven sorceress had a super steady hand with a mascara pencil.

One of the bros told a joke. Ivree lost another few drops of martini to the tabletop. Everybody laughed. Sam joined in, hopefully not too late. Her mind kept drifting back to what Driff had told her the day before. Was there really a secret group of people in charge of maintaining the power of death in territories spread across the globe? She glanced up at an elf dancing on a saucer and decided anything was possible, even Driff's reapers. Still, her father had warned her never to take anything the Council of Intelligence said at face value, and he'd scoffed heavily at her retelling of Driff's activities in Harksburg. Even the Gadukah couldn't verify his claims. The truth, she suspected, was of a similar shape but a wholly different size and color. There was no way Driff had told them the whole story.

"Hanging in there?" Aubin asked. She somehow fought the urge to recoil when his hot breath hit her ear.

"I'm good," she replied. "I'm not that used to clubs. First time." Honesty seemed like the best policy here.

He nodded and smiled. "Explain to me again why you can't drink alcohol until you're twenty-three where you're from."

"Twenty-one," she corrected. "I guess it's because people older than that forgot they could handle it just fine when they were that age."

Aubin leaned back and guffawed. The others, who hadn't heard a word they'd said, looked at them jealously as if they'd been left out. Blue Eyes seemed particularly concerned. Ivree drew their attention away by asking about their workout routines.

"That's funnier than any of your friend's stories," Aubin said.

"I can't tell if you're humoring me or passing judgment on my culture," Sam replied after a helpful bit of painkiller. The part of her that thought immediately downing the whole thing and ordering another would make this whole situation a lot easier to deal with had become obnoxiously loud. That probably meant it was time for a break. "Where's the restroom?"

Aubin pointed to a dimly lit corridor in the corner of the room, to the right of the bar. "Please don't stray long. I'm worried Ivree's going to eat my friends alive."

"That's what she's here for!" Sam replied with a genuine smile and a wink as she slid out the side of the booth. She worried that maybe she'd been too harsh with Aubin, but she doubted a little bit of snark would make him rethink anything nefarious he had planned.

The pendant linking Sam back to her home was a comfortable weight around her neck as she stepped off the platform and onto the busy main floor. Without it, she never would've left Ivree's side—but making herself a target was sort of the plan. Every member of Team Brooks was convinced that Aubin's invitation for a night out came with a heaping helping of devious intentions. Roger and Talora thought he'd try to turn her against them. Driff and Hirace suspected something worse. Ivree was adamant he just wanted to get in Sam's pants as some sort of weird fuck you to his father. Regardless, they needed intel, and so it was decided that Sam should accept Aubin's offer, bring an extremely qualified bodyguard capable of tricking the opposition into thinking she's a complete mess, and rely on the transpoint pendant if things got hairy. Sam hated the idea of relying on the magic to get her out of a bad situation, but she couldn't argue with the plan's logic. With Cark missing and Balacath's barrels tagged with Kron the Withered's runes, they needed to know where the Lightning Club stood.

She skirted the dance floor by following a narrow path around the edge defined by glowing green tape. Huge bouncers spaced every thirty feet or so enforced the tape's sovereignty. Most of them ignored her as she hurried past, but a few watched her closely, confused by the sight of a human in their midst. One did a double-take, then nodded, smiled, and offered a high-five when he realized who she was. She slapped his hand happily and continued on, rounding the corner and following the green tape that now kept the dancers from colliding with the elves waiting for a turn at the bar. She wondered briefly if any of the bouncers were in cahoots with Aubin, then dismissed the thought. He wasn't that clever.

As is typical for such establishments, the line for the restroom was about a dozen customers long. Samantha fell in behind a trio of women having an intense, whispered conversation and leaned her shoulder against the cinderblock wall. The thumping beats echoing through the corridor made attaining the little slice of momentary peace she was seeking impossible.

A man exited the restroom. A woman entered. Everyone waiting took a step forward. Once again Sam's mind drifted to the reapers. She wondered how many of them truly stuck to their responsibilities. Driff's Harksburg story suggested they possessed a certain amount of freedom in fulfilling their duties if they could push past the primal urge and searing pain involved. With an intelligence behind it, death could become a much more merciful process. Children wouldn't have to die of illness or accident. The unlucky and the innocent could be granted second chances. A sympathetic reaper in the right territory could make a world of difference, but the sheer number of horrible deaths in the world told her just how rare that was.

Likewise, if Driff's theory was right, a compromised reaper would be a huge problem.

The line moved again. A short man in lace and purple glitter stumbled past on his way back to the dance floor, his pupils dilated out to the whites by some unknown narcotic. One of the women in front of Sam noticed her.

"Hey," she said warmly, "are you the Pintiri's daughter?"

Sam nodded. "And his Chief of Staff."

The elf's two companions turned to get a look. Sam wasn't particularly in the mood to chat, but she knew her position required it—and maybe these three would turn out to be a nice break from Aubin and the meatheads.

"Rot," the redhead said, "that sounds like a tough job."

"You look like you'd rather be in bed, reading a book," the brunette said.

"Is it that obvious I don't want to be here?" Sam asked.

"Nobody actually *wants* to hang out in places like this," the first one, the blonde, said. "I only put up with it because I like the booze and the music."

"I like the people watching," the redhead said.

"I'm praying one of those assholes dancing on the saucers falls off," the brunette said to a round of laughter.

Sam realized then that the women were triplets. They had the same almond-shaped eyes, the same strong jaws, and the same smattering of freckles across their cheeks. They appeared to be wearing pieces and parts of the same three outfits, mixed and matched between the them into a style Sam could only describe as "party secretary." She liked it. There was no telling which of the three—if any—had retained her natural hair color.

"We know," the blonde said, "we're sisters!"

"Hey, I didn't rag on you for realizing the only human girl in here is the Pintiri's daughter."

That triggered another round of laughter. It felt good. Maybe the night wouldn't be a total loss.

"What're you in for, Miss Brooks?" the redhead asked.

Sam took a few moments to consider her answer. "I've been tasked with entertaining a boy who's probably up to no good in the hopes he'll slip up so we can bring him in."

"Been there, done that," the brunette replied with a flip of her hair. "Older businessman. Total shithead."

"Not me, but a good friend of mine," the blonde added. "Little guy with a wooden personality."

The redhead frowned. "I'm probably headed for the same fate, unfortunately. Got a consulting gig lined up at a company with some serious management issues."

"Got any advice for me?" Sam asked.

"Go for his wallet," the brunette said.

"Go for his balls!" the blonde chirped.

"Go home," the redhead said with a wink.

"I was thinking I'd go to the bathroom first," Sam replied.

"Social engineering is best performed on an empty bladder," the brunette said thoughtfully.

"Don't touch the seat," the blonde added.

"Go ahead of us," the redhead offered, motioning to the door.

Sam hadn't realized that their little clique had reached the front of the line. "You sure?" she asked.

"Get in there," the brunette said. "You've got a big night ahead of you."

"We'll look you up," the blonde promised. "The Pintiri's address isn't some big state secret."

The redhead put a reassuring hand on Samantha's shoulder. "And remember: you've got this. That boy doesn't know who he's messing with."

Samantha's body filled with warm confidence. "Thank you," she said as she brushed past them. "Nice to meet you all!"

"Nice to meet you too!" the blonde and the redhead said in unison. The brunette was half a beat behind, probably intentionally.

Sam had never been in a unisex bathroom before, but compared to all the other new things she'd done in the last week it didn't even register as a novelty. She brushed past an older man in a toga primping himself in the mirror and eased into a narrow stall. The graffiti covering the cheap wooden interior reminded her of the runes on the city wall. She eyed them suspiciously, worried some of the symbols she couldn't decipher were enabling someone to watch her or worse, then dismissed it and went about her business. She was delighted to discover that someone had written "Driff stinks!" in thick black marker on the back of the door.

Afterward, she lingered by the mirror, pretending to fix her hair and hoping she'd run into the triplets again. They were nowhere to be found in the steady stream of elves moving through that restroom, nor were they in the corridor outside. Either the three could pee amazingly fast or they'd had to leave. Sam couldn't bring herself to be suspicious of them. It felt wrong somehow, like trying to put on a pair of pants that were a couple sizes too big.

Blue Eyes was waiting for her at the corner. She hadn't realized just how tall he was until she saw him leaning there against the wall. He pushed himself into the center of the hallway to block her path. "Buy you a drink?" he asked.

She pretended to think about it for a few seconds. "Depends. Does your offer still stand if I admit I don't remember your name?"

His eyes twinkled. "It does, but now it's limited to beer or well liquor only."

Sam traced the line of his strong chin and wondered how she would've felt about him if she didn't know he was up to something. "Good enough for me."

He stepped aside and motioned her forward. "I'm Albie."

"I'm thirsty." Sam hated herself.

They joined the horde waiting for service at the bar. Being packed so tightly among so many people was one of Sam's least favorite things. Her arm was pressed against Albie's, but she couldn't separate herself without giving the slender woman on her opposite side a rather rude shove. No one else seemed to mind, so she decided to try to take it in stride.

A man covered in what appeared to be rainbow sprinkles brushed past carrying two bright green highballs, bumping Sam into Albie. She decided to cut through the awkwardness with conversation. "Let me guess: third base?"

"Shortstop, actually," Albie replied. His eyes sparkled. She wished she knew if that effect was natural or magical so she could properly judge how much to despise it. "Are you a fan of the game?"

"I enjoy it when I see it, but I don't seek it out!" She felt like she had to scream to be heard above the bass. "Dad tried to get me into it, but it didn't really stick!"

"We'll have to get you two out to a game, then." Why did so many elven boys insist on dragging her all around town? "The Pintiri's got a permanent pair of box seats right beside the first base dugout. Front row."

"Don't tell my father about those! He'll never get anything done!"

Albie chuckled. His eyes glittered as he looked at her expectantly. "Oh, right. You don't know his predecessors. Talk of a Pintiri getting things done is usually sarcastic."

That legitimately piqued Samantha's interest. "I've heard Rotreego was...interesting!"

They took a step forward. Only two rows stood between them and the bar.

"Rotreego was a useless, womanizing prick," Albie replied with unmistakeable venom.

"I take it he wasn't a baseball fan!"

"Here's the thing with Pintiris: they talk a big game, and they're always around to take all the credit, but the Mongan and the Council and the Gadukah and a zillion other people who don't get box seats do all the real work." His eye color went flat. Magic, then. "The only thing they're usually good for is pointing that Ether in the right direction. Sometimes even that's too much to ask of them."

"I didn't know that!"

He shook his head. When he looked at her again, his eyes shimmered. "You're new. No one expects you to." He hesitated. "My father was Gadukah. Rynes's lieutenant. A veteran of over three dozen successful combat missions under Rotreego. Dad hated his fucking guts."

Sam didn't get the impression Albie was lying. There was too much raw, genuine emotion pouring out of him. His formerly straight posture had turned into a slouch. His eyes were bright not because of magic but because of sadness. Sam was pretty sure she knew how this story was going to end. Her heart dropped into her stomach and she suddenly felt guilty for allowing Ivree to accompany her that night.

"I'm sorry," she said, grasping his bicep reassuringly.

"It's fine," he said. "Rot, I told Aubin something like this might happen."

And Aubin knew he could use it to his advantage. Still, she had to ask. "What happened?"

"Trolls were causing trouble in Helsinki," he said. Sam almost couldn't hear him, and she had to read his lips to decipher a few syllables. "Tallisker put a cool mil on the leader's head. Rotreego— who already had the run of Evitankari, mind you—dragged the Gadukah with him. They can't say no. So the Pintiri, the Mongan, and six Gadukah step into a Helsinki slum. Three hundred magically disguised trolls decloak all at once. The elven forces beat a hasty retreat...but they never would've made it to the extraction point without the man who stayed behind."

Three feet of empty space opened up between the two of them and the bar. They reflexively filled it. A bartender with a long, looping braid appeared on the other side of the granite and demanded their attention. "What'll you have?" She wilted a bit when she saw the grim expression on Albie's face.

"Two shots of your best whiskey," Sam squeaked. "And then I'll take a painkiller, and this guy gets whatever he wants—all on the Pintiri's tab." She pointed to her ears as proof. The bartender nodded and smiled.

"Dragon's breath for me," Albie said. He turned to Samantha as the bartender darted away to fill their order. "And thank you. That's more than Rotreego ever did for my Pop."

Sam decided to change the subject before she lost her composure. "What's in a dragon's breath?"

His eyes lit up. "That's just what they call the house margarita. Remember which asshole financed this place?"

Sam laughed, louder and harder than she had with the triplets. If only that night had occurred under better circumstances. Aubin was probably a filthy snake, but maybe his taste in establishments wasn't so bad after all. "Any good?"

"They use the cheapest tequila they can find, but it's still the best in town."

"Can't be better than Aubin's legendary antifreeze."

Albie's eyes went supernova. "Tastes better, but it won't kill the dog if you accidentally leave it on the table."

The bartender reappeared, clearly relieved to see the two of them laughing. She carried a pair of shots in her right hand and levitated their other drinks above her left. "Our regards to your father, Miss Brooks!" she chirped as she set the whole load down and moved on to her next customer.

For a moment Sam looked down at the shots as if they were hand grenades. It was possible, given the circumstances, that drinking straight liquor was a bad idea, but it was too late now. She snatched up the glasses and offered one to Albie. "To your father."

"And yours," he replied. He saluted her with his shot and then knocked it back.

Sam returned the gesture. That was only her third time drinking straight whiskey, but she realized later that it was also her favorite. The oaky taste and gentle burn steeled her nerves. She could take care of Aubin and solve the case of the missing heads. No problem!

And then, she decided, she'd insist that her father see to it that Albie's family was well taken care of.

He grabbed her painkiller and his margarita and motioned for her to lead the way back. Sam was annoyed to find Aubin waiting for them in the aisle.

"I was beginning to worry you'd fallen in," he said with a wry grin.

Part of Sam wished she had. "I made a friend," she said nonchalantly.

Albie handed Sam her drink and continued back toward the table. Aubin watched him go, his lips pursed in suspicion. When Albie was out of sight, he leaned close to Sam and grabbed her wrist. "You probably shouldn't drink that. Albie has a reputation."

Samantha seriously doubted that, and hearing Aubin slander his supposed friend as the climax of his manipulation almost made her head explode. Rage boiled up from the pit of her stomach, buoyed by liquor and focused by the triplets' encouragement. Nothing would've made her happier than slapping the fake concern right out of his face, kicking him in the balls, lifting his wallet, and going home—but that would compromise the whole operation and cause no end of situations more obnoxious than this one. Her father would be disappointed. Driff would be insufferable. And they'd be no closer to understanding just what in the heck was going on.

She directed her disgust toward the painkiller, hoping she looked shocked and disappointed. "Okay."

"Let's get some air," Aubin suggested, yanking her toward the bathroom hallway.

His iron grip on her wrist told Sam that her camp's worst fears had been spot on. She followed along in a daze, mentally frozen in place. The cool contents of her drink sloshed all over her hand. A week and a half ago she'd been just an average college student with a fractured family. Life had been uncomfortable, but it was also probably going to turn out perfectly fine. She never had to worry about anything more dangerous than crossing a busy street. Being dragged outside a strange dance club by a large male of a different species who obviously meant to use her for his family's own gain was beyond anything she'd ever faced.

As they rounded the corner, she once again found herself looking for the triplets. They'd help. They'd recognize Aubin's intentions, surround him like a pack of wolves, and proceed to tear him a new asshole—physically, or perhaps magically, if verbally didn't get the job done. None of the booze-addled or drugged-out elves in line were the triplets, and none of them realized what was happening. Sam was too stunned to call out for help.

Aubin traded friendly nods with a bouncer as he pushed outside through an emergency exit. The sign warning about an alarm was a lie. Exiting into the warm, slightly humid night air was a shock to Sam's system, and it took a moment for her vision to adjust to actual darkness. They'd stepped out into a small nook carved into the back of the building to store a dumpster and a couple pallets of nondescript crates. A familiar figure leaned against the far wall, flanked by a similarly familiar blue garbage barrel.

Dash opened the lid. "It's going to hurt, but it won't kill you." He seemed wrong somehow. Slumped. Chagrined. Defeated. The exact opposite of the character she knew from the books, and a shell of the quiet but seemingly confident man she'd come to know. Something terrible had gotten to him—and Sam bet whatever it was waited for her on the other side of the black hole in that barrel.

Go for his wallet.

Go for his balls.

Go home.

And don't forget: you've got this. That boy doesn't know who he's messing with!

She knew what she had to do. "Mind if I finish my drink first?"

The glass shattered easily against Aubin's skull. Liquor supernova-ed across the alley. Sam barely noticed the shards embedded in her hand. Aubin lost his grip on her wrist and stumbled backward, gritting his teeth and hissing in pain.

Samantha sprung forward and tackled the surprised Dash before he could react, wrapping her arms around his torso on the way down. She mostly landed on top of him, but her elbow slammed hard against the pavement. Her forearms screamed under their combined weight. She ignored it and focused on a single word.

Home.

Triggering the pendant was nothing at all like she imagined— which is to say the act itself was so sudden she had no time to register she'd done it. One moment she was on top of Dash in a dirty alley, the next she was on top of Dash on a familiar carpet. People made surprised sounds. Dash swore.

Sam rolled away and collided with an end table. Balacath—of all people—helped her to her feet. "I just got here," he said shyly. "I wanted to warn you that someone had stolen one of my barrels. I assume this is the culprit?"

Three people were pointing dangerous weapons down at the shaken elf she'd dragged through the transpoint network: Driff with his silver six-shooter, Talora with hands burning with magical fire, and her father with the most powerful shotgun in the world.

"This is the part where you tell me what the fuck you want with my fucking daughter," Roger snarled. Sam had never been so proud of him.

— CHAPTER SIXTEEN —

Dash wanted to die.

He'd given Driff and the Pintiri pretty much everything. He told them about the barrels and about Cark, Chyve, and Aldern. He told them Aubin had zeroed in on Samantha at his father's behest, and that he'd foolishly tried to use that to his advantage to fulfill Aldern's request using the same barrel Lesryn had thrown him into. He hadn't bothered trying to apologize. After issuing a few vague threats about what would happen if they discovered he was lying, they threw Dash in a cell.

There were, of course, things he hadn't mentioned, primarily concerning why Aldern had sought his help in the first place. He knew he'd be forced to reveal that information soon enough, and he knew how Keighlan would react when she inevitably found out, and he'd spent the last few hours since breakfast trying to figure out how to off himself. The guards hadn't left him with shoelaces or a belt, and the elastic waistband of his orange jumpsuit didn't seem up to the task, so hanging was out of the question. The tiny puddle of water in the silver toilet wouldn't make drowning easy. He couldn't face plant off the floor-bound mattress, bang his head against the padded walls, or choke himself between the magically electrified bars. He'd already tried that last one. It had thrown him across the room and into the aforementioned cushioning.

Defeated and desperate, he'd curled into a ball atop the mattress and wedged himself as deep into the corner as possible. He cursed Granger and the stupid fucking offer they should've turned down. He cursed Aldern for always being a manipulative shithead. He cursed Samantha Brooks for being too fucking clever for her own fucking good. He considered his own relevant decisions, made so long ago when he was so young and then again recently while under considerable duress, and gave himself a pass.

Keighlan appeared on the other side of the bars. At first Dash thought he was imagining her. He'd never seen his wife look so detached. The black jacket, skirt, and heels made it clear she meant business, and she'd pulled her hair back into the sort of severe bun that promised the wrath of hell upon anyone who challenged her. She glanced at him once, fire in her eyes, and then shifted her attention to a spot on the concrete floor. She didn't say hello or ask her husband how he was doing. Dash's heart broke.

Samantha Brooks strode into view and wrapped a protective arm around Keighlan. Her hand was wrapped in a bandage and she looked like she hadn't slept. White hot hatred flared to life in Dash's chest. Satisfying fantasies of reaching out through the hexed bars to snap her neck danced through his subconscious. He blamed Samantha for his fate more than anyone. Everything had been fine before that bitch and her father had shown up.

"Tell me what really happened," Keighlan croaked.

"Hi, K," Dash replied sadly.

"Tell me what really happened, you fucking asshole!"

Her tone cut right through Dash and somehow made him collapse in upon himself even further. "Aldern recruited me to abduct the Brooks children in Balacath's stead—"

"Balacath was never involved," she snarled, "and I know all about what you tried to pull last night. Tell me what happened before."

"Before what?"

She took a deep breath, composing herself. "Why did Aldern recruit you?"

There it was. "Opportunity," he lied. "Out of the four of us, I was the most out of my element in my job as Council of Agriculture. That made it easy. I was set up."

She shook her head and put her hands over her eyes.

Dash sensed a crack. He stood up. "K, you have to believe me. Granger set me up to fail. What the fuck do I know about farming? He put me in an uncomfortable position where Aldern's agents could get to me whenever they wanted. Find Lesryn and Corken. They'll know more."

"We tried. They're gone," Samantha snapped. "Aldern could've targeted any of the Lightning Club members the way you described. Why you?"

Rot damned troll fucking demon spawn Samantha fucking Brooks. "Stay out of this, human," Dash snarled. "This is none of your business and you shouldn't fucking be here."

"I asked her to come," Keighlan said steadily, "because I knew she wouldn't let you get to me. Now tell me the truth: why did Aldern recruit you? And why did you go through with it? What leverage does he have over you? Rot, Dash, you tried to abduct the Pintiri's daughter last night! Aldern's got something, or you would've never..."

He'd dreaded this moment for decades. It had kept him awake at night and driven his blood pressure through the roof. It was the stuff of his most horrific nightmares. Worst of all, Keighlan knew something was wrong primarily because she'd always had faith in him. She was right; he never would've done something so heinous if he'd had any other choice. The thought broke him. "I could tell you, but you wouldn't be able to process it. The dust won't let you."

Keighlan raised one eyebrow as she dramatically drew a loaded syringe from her pants pocket. Dash recognized its stumpy shape and red plunger immediately. He watched helplessly as she knelt, jabbed herself in the ankle, and injected the terrifying black solution into her veins.

"Where'd you get that?" Dash asked in awe.

"I'm the Council of Medicine, remember?"

"What the hell was it?" Samantha asked, aghast.

Keighlan leaned back into a sitting position against the wall. Samantha crouched beside her, clearly concerned. "Perambyrol. The dust creates barriers blocking off unwanted memories. Breaking those barriers releases a deadly poison, but combined with this stuff it becomes a harmless substance passed in urine. Of course, perambyrol itself is usually fatal, so we better hope there's a few narii colonies in my head. Supposedly the fear of impending death makes them easier to break. Guess we'll see." She shrugged. "Start talking, D. I've got three minutes, maybe four, before this crap stops my heart. I'm not sure. I'm not very good at this Council of Medicine stuff."

Samantha sprung to her feet. "I'll go get help."

Keighlan grabbed her wrist. "No. There is no antidote, other than what's in my head. Stay. Please."

Samantha nodded and sat back down beside Keighlan. Dash couldn't have been more jealous. That should've been him there beside his wife in her last moments.

"Talk," Keighlan insisted.

"No," he croaked. "I'd rather watch you die than see you hate me." The words burned his throat like acid.

She laughed. "In case you can't tell, I really fucking hate you right now—and I can't feel my toes."

Dash shook his head. Tears streamed down his face. "You're done with me either way."

"So you're just going to let your wife die?" Samantha asked in disbelief. "You're an asshole."

I'm much worse than that, he thought. And given what had already been done to Keighlan, how bad was a quick death, really? The truth would tear her apart. Dash locked his gaze to hers, thinking it was the least he could do for her as she faded away. Rot, she had such beautiful eyes.

The unmistakeable staccato of high heels on concrete echoed through the corridor. Samantha and Keighlan both looked to their left. More than one person was approaching, if Dash wasn't mistaken, and they were arriving quickly. Not that it would make a difference.

Samantha's jaw dropped. "Oh, what the fuck..."

"The power of love didn't defeat Kron the Withered," three female voices said, mostly in unison. One was just a beat behind the other two. "I did!"

"What?" Keighlan asked, confused. "I saw it myself. The love between Lazzy and Gearix powered a spell that broke Kron. Only the four of us were there." Dash nodded weakly, encouraging her confusion.

"Five," the brunette said as she stepped in front of Dash's cell.

"I followed you into Kron's lair," the blonde said.

"I'd been trying to tag along everywhere the Lightning Club went, but you wouldn't let me," the redhead added. "So I had to be sneaky!"

"I don't remember any triplets," Keighlan said, clearly trying very hard to break through the memory walls that might be hiding them. She'd begun sweating and breathing heavily as the perambyrol progressed through her system. Beside her, Samantha stared at the three women in utter shock. She hadn't moved since they'd appeared. Dash wished they'd all go away so he could lament his wife's passing in peace.

There was a blinding flash. When it dissipated, the triplets were gone. Standing in their place was a slender elven woman with alabaster skin and long dark hair. A black dress hung loosely from her bony shoulders. Intelligence—and something very sad—twinkled in her heavy eyes. Dash felt like he knew her, but he couldn't place her.

"The Witch!" Samantha gasped, clutching desperately at a pendant around her neck.

Rayn. Powerful, mysterious agent of chaos. Unpredictability, manipulative nature, and general lack of social awareness makes her unwelcome pretty much everywhere.

A brief hint of recognition lit up Keighlan's face, then faded as a convulsion wracked her body. Dash vomited all over himself. This was really it, then. He didn't even have the energy to beg Keighlan not to listen.

Rayn knelt beside Dash's wife. "That's right," she said softly. "My name is Rayn. I was Headmaster Aldern's apprentice."

Keighlan frowned, forcing herself to fight off the pain so she could make herself remember. "Aldern had an apprentice? That doesn't make sense. Academy staff don't take on apprentices. That's not how things work. We all go through classes the same way..."

"I was the most powerful student Aldern had ever seen, so he took me under his wing." The Witch smiled in a way that could've melted the paint off the walls. "The other students all hated me, you four especially. Maybe it was jealousy, or maybe just typical teenage bullshit. You'll remember, when we get through this. Regardless, when Aldern disappeared, I was the first person the Lightning Club suspected."

Keighlan took a deep, raspy breath. The perambyrol had to be into her thigh, if not further. "That's...maybe? Our first suspect was Bug Eyes Betta, the girl Aldern put in detention every day."

"Me. Or a version of me, whipped up to fool you and make the books more interesting. I offered to aid you in your search, because I knew you had information I didn't. Lazzy refused, and Dash threatened to report me to the academic board if you caught me following you."

Keighlan blinked. "Dash hit Bug Eyes Betta with a piece of cake at the ball."

Rayn sighed. "Also me. It was chocolate and it didn't taste good. Now focus: after you defeated Balacath and entered Kron's lair through the rune on the blackboard—"

"We found Aldern. Kron had almost killed him!"

"Lazzy stepped up..."

"...and called me to his side, thinking he could use what we'd learned from the fairy queen about the power of love to stop Kron. I rejected him." Keighlan stopped. Her eyes widened. "No. No, I didn't. I loved Lazzy."

Dash's heart broke.

"I've loved Lazzy since we were little kids," Keighlan continued. Her eyes darted about as if she were trying to make sense of the data on three or four different computer screens. The walls blocking her memories were collapsing, and the perambyrol would soon be neutralized by the resulting chemical release. "I kissed him in Willowglen when we were ten. I slow danced with him at the ball after he broke Balacath's spell. He loved me, and I loved him, and together..."

"Kron almost killed you too," Rayn said. "There was no power of love. You were just two brave kids who wanted to go down fighting, while Dash and Gearix cowered around the corner."

"You followed us into Kron's lair. You stopped him right before he was about to finish us off. Aldern didn't take Kron's medallion—you did. And when you tried to run off with it..."

Keighlan's eyes turned ice cold and settled on the quivering heap of flesh that was all that remained of her husband. "Dash sucker punched you."

"Kron was the rightful guardian of that medallion," Rayn continued. "As Aldern's apprentice, I knew it could unleash Axzar from his imprisonment in Tash Square—and that my master was too much of a piece of shit to be trusted with it."

Keighlan snarled like a predatory animal. "I remember that. Aldern begged you to hand it over, and you told him exactly what you just told us and took off. My asshole husband thought he could gain the Headmaster's favor by stopping you, and he did. Lazzy, Gearix, Balacath, and I were all dusted—and I was Dash's fucking reward."

She leapt to her feet. Lightning crackled across her hands as she summoned her magic. "He was dating Gearix, but he'd always thought she wasn't pretty enough. The dust rewrote our history in my mind and made me love him. He took what Balacath had done to me and created something even worse. My entire life has been a lie."

Dash didn't care. There was nothing left in his mind that could register any of these words as more than pure information. His life was effectively over, whether Keighlan took it from him in anger or not.

She let the magic in her palms fizzle out and turned to the Witch. "Dash knew all this. Why did Aldern let him keep his memories?"

"Leverage. Aldern knows a useful rube when he sees one, and he knew that what happened in Kron's lair would be relevant again someday. Giving Dash the thing he wanted most and leaving him to remember he'd achieved it through a terrible act gave Aldern complete control. No one would've believed Dash if he'd come forward with the real story, especially with the rest of you denying it." Rayn looked down to Samantha and smiled mischievously. "Aldern got Dash's balls and his wallet and went home."

The girl recoiled. "If you knew all this, why didn't you come out and tell us at the beginning?"

"Would you have believed me?"

"No."

"If I had told you there was something fishy about the Lightning Club instead of leaving that extraordinarily well-designed book cover in your bedroom to make you suspicious, would you have believed me?"

"No, and stay out of my room."

"Would you have accepted my encouragement in the bar last night?"

"No."

"Would you have believed me if I told you there's a seemingly immortal cadre of elves pulling the strings of all the secret magic people who think they're the ones really dictating the course of history?"

"No."

"And if I'd told you that Aldern wants you and your brother because one of you is carrying what's left of Axzar's soul..."

— CHAPTER SEVENTEEN —

Keighlan shuffled meekly into Merrowood's living room. She'd spent the last half hour upstairs, examining Ricky in his bedroom. "It's your son," Keighlan announced sadly. "I think."

Samantha had never felt more relieved, and yet—that meant her brother was harboring the millennia-old soul of the most evil demon lord to ever walk the face of the earth. The trade-off wasn't exactly fair. She leaned back into the plush couch and closed her eyes, wishing for a way to turn back the clock and avoid all of this.

"Motherfucker!" Roger snarled, bolting out of his favorite recliner. Sam had never seen her father so angry.

Talora wrapped her arms around him. "I'm sorry, my love. We'll figure this out." That calmed Roger, but he still looked ready to pounce.

"Samantha, you're sure there's nothing else you can tell us?" Driff asked. His voice broke ever so slightly. He was just as freaked out as the rest of them, which normally would've warmed Sam's heart—but not here.

"Rayn disappeared immediately," Sam muttered, choking down what would've been her fourth angry rebuttal of that question. "What do we do about Ricky?"

Keighlan shook her head. "He seems stable enough for now. This is way beyond my experience. We need more information, but I don't have even the slightest idea where to start." She took a deep breath. "I have to apologize to you all. If the Lightning Club hadn't gotten involved all those years ago, Aldern might never have stolen Kron's amulet, and Ricky..."

"This is not your fault," Roger said quickly. "That fucking Witch needs to stop fucking with my fucking family." He leered threateningly at Driff as if punching the target of his anger's former lackey would make him feel a lot better.

"Yes, she does," the Council of Intelligence agreed. "Right now, we need to plan our response. Aldern will know that Dash's attempt to kidnap Samantha failed. He will try again."

Walinda flittered into the living room right on cue. "Executive Director Cark requests the Pintiri's presence at the morgue. He suggests you bring—and I quote—the whole family."

Roger patted the shotgun at his hip. "It'll just be me and Betsy here."

"Sure," Driff said. "Go ahead and shoot him. Then shoot him again tomorrow, then the day after that, then the day after that, and the day after that..."

"Sounds fun to me, but I get your point."

"We need to change the game," Driff said. "We need to trick them somehow so we can buy the time we need to come up with something better."

"How the fuck do we do that?"

Talora tapped her chin thoughtfully. "We call in a few favors from people they won't expect."

— CHAPTER EIGHTEEN —

Dash still wanted to die, and now he was worried it would never, ever happen.

"Aldern will be so glad to see you again!" Cark screeched. The strange elf sat cross-legged atop an examining table in the center of the morgue beside one of Port's blue barrels. The pair of guards who'd spirited Dash out of his cell were long gone. The strange fire that had kept the place frigid during his previous visit had been put out, rendering the room a bit stuffy.

"Nothing to say for yourself?" Cark asked.

Dash, in fact, didn't have anything to say. Lazzy's once-spirited sidekick was completely broken. His surroundings made sense as inputs but generated little or no conscious reaction. His body was on autopilot as his mind wallowed in the abyss into which he'd plunged when Keighlan regained her memories. Some small part of him realized he should've felt remorse or regret for his actions, but that voice was drowned out by his overwhelming need to bring it all to an end. There was no coming back from this.

Cark drummed his fingers against the side of the examination table. "You know, it's rare that we forgive those who fail us, and rarer still that we don't just murder those liabilities immediately!

Aldern's either attached to you, or he's got something really special in mind!"

Dash continued staring at the floor. The morgue's staff kept the place spotless, but the deep scratches in the linoleum betrayed their lack of a budget for really taking care of the place. His eyes slowly traced a pair of criss-crossing gouges that looked like a sickle.

"You just don't get it, do you?" Cark continued. "We've got millennia of practice at this! You're what, thirty-five? We've had disagreements that lasted ten times that! You are statistically insignificant! Six centuries from now I'll be sitting in the virtual reality room with Aldern and Lesryn and I'll say 'Hey, guys! Do you remember that nobody who couldn't do that thing we asked him to do with those weird garbage cans?' and they'll say 'No, Cark! Which nobody? There were so many nobodies! We couldn't possibly keep track of them all!'"

Tracing the faux grout lines in between the linoleum's tiles was a struggle. Something in the pattern kept trying to force Dash's eyes to cross. He gave in and let it happen. Identical slices of cheap flooring swirled through and across each other in his vision, perhaps as a metaphor for Cark's rambling dismissal of the mortal. Dash was ambivalent about this thought.

Cark, however, couldn't handle being ignored. He slid down off the examination table, stomped over to Dash, took firm hold of the other elf's face, and jerked his attention up from the floor. "You're nothing!" Cark declared. Hatred burned in his manic eyes as he squeezed Dash's lips together. "We are the Eternal, you fucking maggot, and your life means nothing to us!"

Before Dash could realize that he still didn't care, someone cleared his throat.

"Hi," Roger Brooks said from just inside the entrance. "I was told you wanted to see me." He held his shotgun low in both hands, ready to raise it to a firing position. A little boy—Ricky,

Dash assumed—clung to his hip. Council of Intelligence Driff and Commander Rynes flanked father and son.

Cark released Dash, smoothed his shirt, and stood up straight. "Good of you to come, Pintiri!" he said with a slick smile. "I believe, however, that I invited your entire brood!"

"It's the boy," Roger said sadly. He tousled Ricky's thick mop of hair affectionately.

"Ah. Well, you know we'll be back—and we'll be very unhappy— if it isn't!"

"I know." Roger hesitated, clearly nervous and perhaps a bit embarrassed. "Thing is...I need your help. I want this thing out of my son. If anyone can make that happen, it's Aldern."

Cark nodded. "You're not wrong! The man does amazing things! And allow me to reassure you that it's not your son we want: it's the ancient demon lord riding along inside of him!"

"Yeah, well, that'd better be the truth," Roger said. "There's one more thing I need to be sure about, though."

After a few seconds of awkward silence, Cark took a step forward and spread his arms wide. "What is it, Pintiri?"

Roger smiled. "Ricky, don't look."

The boy buried his face in his father's jeans. Roger snapped his shotgun up into position and pulled the trigger. The weapon roared as its side-by-side barrels belched a pair of bright blue fireballs. Cark began rolling his eyes just as the blast blew apart his left side in a burst of blood and flesh. The force of the blow spun him around and threw him back into the examination table. He bounced off and landed face-first on the ground. Blood and organs oozed out onto the floor from through the ragged wound. The Ether-fueled shot continued on its way and tore a jagged hole in the morgue's wall.

"Asshole," Driff muttered as he wiped a few specks of blood off his spectacles.

"I told you I was going to shoot him," Roger deadpanned as he brushed a few spots of Cark off his own jacket with his sleeve. "Some Council of Intelligence you are."

"Can I look yet, Daddy?" Ricky asked.

"Absolutely not."

Dash had caught the worst of it, but he lacked the motivation to bother with the gooey Cark bits covering his clothes, face and hair. He supposed the bit of intestine dangling from the end of his nose could've been considered morbidly humorous. "Me next?" he asked so softly no one heard.

Several tense moments passed. Cark remained dead.

"Maybe blasting him immediately wasn't such a bad idea after all," Roger said.

"Patience," Driff replied. "This usually takes a few seconds."

The scattered Cark chunks began to quiver. The exceptionally odd sensation of fleshy bits wriggling across his skin almost spurred Dash into action. Drops of Cark's blood rose a few inches off whatever they were stuck to and hovered in the air.

"That's disconcerting," Rynes said, clearly fighting the urge to gag.

All at once, the important bits that had been inside the morgue's director zoomed back into his body. Pale, sickly looking flesh swirled together to shut the wound. Some sort of internal heat flushed the new skin red, then it faded back to pink. Cark's body shook and popped as if he were being electrified. When it stopped, a soft moan eased out from between his lips.

"Aldern warned me you might do that," Cark said as he rolled over onto his back. "'No,' I told him, 'our noble Pintiri would never debase himself by shooting a harmless messenger!' Rot, that hurts even worse than when the Ether's carried in a blade." He pulled himself up into a sitting position and blinked a few times.

"I believe it all now," Roger said. "Please help my son...and, uh, sorry I shot you."

Cark used the examination table to pull himself to his feet and then inspected the hole in his shirt. His skin bulged outward as something underneath adjusted itself. "Does the boy have any allergies we should know about?"

Roger shook his head and patted Ricky's shoulder. The enormity of what he was about to do settled over him, draining the color from his face and the steel from his shoulders. Tears welled up in his eyes. He handed his shotgun to Rynes and knelt to face his son. "It's time to go, okay?"

Tears streamed down the boy's face. "I don't want to go with the ugly man," Ricky sobbed.

His father took firm hold of his shoulders and looked him square in the eye. "Cark will bring you to someone who can help you: Aldern, one of Daddy's...old friends."

"I know, but I'm scared."

Roger took a deep breath. "I am too, Ricky, but we have to be brave right now. I told you about the thing they need to fix? The thing that's been making you mean?"

Ricky sobbed. "I don't want to hurt anyone."

"I know. I know you don't. And Cark and Aldern will make sure of it."

Dash didn't dare guess at what the Eternal really had in mind, but he doubted it would be as benevolent as the Brooks family was hoping. His own experience with Aldern's bargains had taught him that much. He clenched his fists and took a short step forward, trying to summon the courage to warn Roger...but then the darkness took over, and his muscles relaxed, and he went back to not caring. Ricky's fate meant nothing to him.

"Okay," Ricky said, wiping snot from his little nose. "Okay. Take care of Mommy and Sam for me?"

Roger wrapped his son in a crushing hug. "You'd better believe it." The little boy struggled to get his arms around his father, clutching desperately at his sides. They stayed like that for a long time.

Dash thought back to his and Keighlan's own decision to delay having kids. Elven conception wasn't as easy as it was among humans, but their increased lifetimes meant they remained fertile significantly longer. Having a child hadn't felt right, even when Gearix became pregnant with Aubin almost immediately after she'd married Lazzy. Keighlan had said she wanted some time with her husband first. Dash had seconded that opinion, although deep down he just hadn't wanted to involve a child in the mess he'd created. Maybe his opinion would've changed if something had happened to Aldern, or if their lives had changed significantly. He supposed now he'd never know. The list of things that had been snatched away from him continued to grow.

Roger and Ricky separated. The little boy bravely walked up to Cark. "I'm ready to go now."

The slimy elf smiled and opened the lid of the garbage can. "After you, then."

Ricky climbed up onto the examination table, looked down at the singularity inside the blue barrel, and turned back to his father for assurance. "It's really dark in there," the boy said.

Roger swallowed hard. "It's just a cloud," he replied, his voice cracking slightly. "It'll take you to visit a nice old wizard who can help you. It's magic."

The boy wasn't convinced. "Sam hates magic."

And Aldern's not a nice old wizard, Dash thought.

"Sam uses magic when she needs to," Roger said, "because she's very brave."

That seemed to steel his son's resolve. Ricky stood up a little straighter and forced a smile. "I can be brave too, like Sam. Bye, Dad."

"See you soon, son."

Ricky stepped out over the black hole and immediately disappeared as the singularity's crushing gravity pulled him inside.

Roger exhaled violently and snatched his weapon back from Rynes. His face flushed red with anger. "Cark, I fucking swear: if you don't bring my son back in one piece, I will find you, I will lock your ass in the tiniest fucking cell I can fucking find, and I will blow you into pieces every four hours every day for the rest of my life."

The elf pressed a hand to his chest. "Pintiri, you have my personal assurance that you've made the correct decision! One of our *many* remaining operatives here in Evitankari will be in touch periodically to update you on the boy's progress!" He turned toward the barrel, then hesitated as if he'd forgotten something. "And if you behave yourself, there might be a few ways to solve your Ether problem so you and your lovely family can go home! We do know a thing or two about cheating death, after all!"

For a moment Roger stared blankly in shock, and then his eyes narrowed. "Gotcha," he snarled.

"Then I bid you all farewell for now!" Cark said with a dramatic bow. Upon rising, he turned to Dash. "After you!"

This, Dash knew, would likely be his last chance to do something about his situation. Once he went through that singularity, his life would be in Aldern's hands. His existence would likely continue far longer than he wanted it to, and it wasn't likely to be comfortable. He decided it would be best to get it over with quickly.

He charged the Pintiri. His legs felt as if they were fighting through mud; every step was a battle, as if his body were fighting his mind's power over it. Still, he closed the gap quickly. Rynes and Driff tensed, both ready to defend the human. Roger took a step forward and motioned for them to stand down.

Dash couldn't understand why the Pintiri hadn't fired. Why was Roger just letting a crazed lunatic run him down? He decided it didn't matter. Someone would have to do something if he got his hands on the Pintiri's throat. He leapt forward, grasping for Roger's neck.

Roger calmly swung the butt of his shotgun up underneath Dash's chin. The impact cracked his jawbone and crushed his teeth together. Blood filled his mouth as he bit into his tongue. The blow stopped him mid-leap, and he felt as if he hung there, suspended and in pain, for an eternity. Perhaps he just wanted that moment to last, so he could wallow in the ultimate culmination of all of his pathetic selfishness. Maybe some part of him realized he was getting exactly what he deserved.

He landed hard on his side and banged his head against the floor. The room around him spun. Roger looked down at him and shook his head. "Tell Aldern I said hello."

Dash desperately worked his bleeding tongue around the inside of his mouth. Maybe he could find a way to choke to death on his own blood.

"Commander Rynes," Roger said smugly, "please take out the trash."

His third trip down the singularity highway hurt just as much as the first two, especially compounded with the agony of his fractured jaw. After landing facedown on the mattress in a way that jarred it even worse, he awkwardly rolled onto his back and waited for his spinning senses to return. His body seemed to be getting used to the effects of regularly being rent into its component atoms and reconstituted; his sight flickered back into place relatively quickly, although he couldn't feel anything below his waist and his upper body felt like it was covered in molasses.

There was something fleshy on the ground beside him. It took a few moments for his maniacally firing brain to realize it was Chyve. Her eyes were wide and lifeless, her jaw slack. A switchblade protruded from her jugular. Blood poured from the wound and pooled around her head.

Cark landed beside Dash, coughing and uttering sounds that sounded vaguely like certain curse words. Dash decided not to warn him about Chyve's condition.

Ricky stepped into view above and behind them. Chyve's blood soaked the boy's face and shirt. At first, Dash thought the demon lord within the boy had taken over, and that he was about to massacre them all and thankfully put an end to his miserable existence. Ricky calmly drew a telescoping wand from his pocket, flicked it open, and pointed it toward the ceiling. Red lightning arced up into the singularity.

Do it, Dash begged, grasping wildly for Cark so he could hold the bastard back if necessary. *End it all.*

A tendril of red lightning burst forth from the garbage barrel, grasping hungrily for something to take hold of. At the Pintiri's command, Balacath strode confidently into the exam room. He flipped open his own wand and met the red magic with a bolt of blue. The two spells flickered across each other above the barrel, then collapsed into each other to form a purple vortex linked back to the two wands by their component colors.

"It's kind of pretty," Roger said. Driff rolled his eyes.

"Now, Pintiri!" Balacath shouted, clearly struggling to control the power involved in the spell. "Shoot it!"

Roger raised his weapon, took careful aim, and fired. Balacath cut off the flow of energy from his wand at the same moment. Twin Ether shots collided with the vortex, swirled around for a moment, and then raced down through the red energy still linked to the singularity, absorbing the lightning as it traveled. There was a loud *wumpf* as it met the black hole, and the sides of the barrel blew out as if someone had set off a small explosive inside.

"Did that work?" Rynes asked.

Balacath bounded forward like a small child rushing to hug a happy puppy. He almost fell into what was left of the barrel as he leaned over its smoking edge to peer down inside. "Success!" he declared. "This singularity's dissipated, and it will have taken all similarly linked singularities with it!"

Roger smiled smugly at Driff and pretended to blow smoke off the end of his shotgun. "What about the people on the other side?" the Council of Intelligence asked.

"Unharmed, as we were."

"How exactly did that work?" Rynes asked. "I'm no physicist, but I'm pretty sure a black hole shouldn't just evaporate like that."

"We created conditions that violated about eighteen fundamental laws of physics and forced that impossible state through the quantum network linking the singularities. The universe cannot allow such contradictions, so everything involved was instantaneously annihilated." Balacath shrugged. "It was the best I could do on two hours' notice."

Rynes smiled. "Sounds pretty damn good to me."

"Well, there was a not statistically insignificant probability of the universe rewriting its core constraints to compensate instead, which would've been very, very bad."

Council of Economics Granger strolled into the room and planted his hands on his wide hips. "That shifter I loaned you led the team to great success, I assume?"

"Great success!" Roger replied. "Please pass my compliments along to your comrade. We couldn't have done it without his stellar performance. That was...uncomfortable."

"Oh, I will. That unit's made it out of tighter scraps than what he just dove into. Hopefully it picks up a few useful secrets during its escape."

"You're planning to share, right?"

"Absolutely! We regret our role in what almost befell your daughter, Pintiri, and I reiterate that we'd previously judged the

Lightning Club to be merely a group of easily exploitable narcissists. We never dreamed they'd become an actual threat."

Driff pushed his spectacles up on his nose. "You should probably reevaluate your risk assessment methods."

Granger chuckled warmly. "You're not wrong. Still, I hope this can lead to a mutually productive partnership."

"As do I!" Roger said faux-officiously. "In fact, there's another matter I could use your help with..."

— CHAPTER NINETEEN —

A slender elf in a red tracksuit guided Ricky Brooks up to the old ship's steering wheel in the center of Port. The elf reached out and placed his free hand on the wheel. Sam's breath caught in her throat as she watched her little brother disappear into the transpoint network for the seventh time that day.

Thankful that was over with, she crossed the final destination off the list on her clipboard. That pair was off to Moscow. The pair prior was headed for a farming commune outside Cheyenne, Wyoming. The pair prior to that were sent to an ex-pat community in downtown London. Seven elven operatives paired with seven shifters shaped like Ricky Brooks had just been dispatched to locations across the globe. From there, they'd link up with two to four more pairs already in the field and scatter through the network once more.

The real Ricky, supposedly, was in there somewhere. Samantha wasn't privy to that information. The fewer people who knew, the better, her father said. She hated not knowing where her brother was. They'd had less than half an hour together to say goodbye. She'd been crying ever since.

Attempting to confuse the Eternal by scattering Rickys across the planet was Talora's idea. Driff had quickly seconded it. Sam had called them both nasty words and vehemently objected. Roger had spent a few minutes thinking it over by himself before agreeing with not-his-wife and the traitor. Sam had called all three of them a few more nasty words before regaining enough of her composure to help.

"It'll just be until we know how to get that thing out of him," Roger had promised. "Believe me, I hate this as much as you do, but we can't possibly protect him here."

Sam didn't believe that for a second. She held out hope that this was some sort of massive swerve, that the real Ricky was sequestered somewhere supremely safe right there in Evitankari. Her father denied it, but in a way that made her suspect he wasn't quite telling the truth.

"That's the last of them," she announced, choking back a sob.

"Obviously," Driff said.

She whirled on him and hurled the clipboard into his chest. "Hey asshole, did you know there were at least seven shifters other than Granger hiding in Evitankari?"

"Enough," Roger declared, forcefully but not without compassion. "This is hard for all of us, but I need both of you if it's going to work."

Samantha bristled at the implication, but held her tongue. "Fine," she said as she accepted her clipboard back from Driff.

"So what's next, now that we've set up the smokescreen?" the Council of Intelligence asked.

Roger sighed. "We need to know why the shala'ni are still dropping Tallisker's towers and find out where both groups stand. Someone has to get to Talvayne to investigate why their transpoint fell off the network. We have to find four new temporary members of the Combined Council, and we need to make sure the elections for their permanent replacements and the Mongan position run smoothly. We need to figure out if the shifters are really on our side or if we're getting played. We need to know where the hell Pike disappeared to. We need to identify any Eternal still active in Evitankari and learn as much as we can about their link to the reapers. We need to determine just what in the fuck the Witch is up to." He hesitated. "And while we're doing all that, we need to learn how to remove the soul of an ancient demon lord from my son."

Samantha had been running a similar list in her own mind, but hearing it all dictated so plainly by her father hammered home not just the enormity of each task but the staggering complexity of it all. "This isn't going to be easy," she said.

"No, it's not," Roger agreed, "but I'm glad you're here at my side to help me get it done." He turned to the Council of Intelligence. "Back before the battle in Old Ev, you promised me something. You haven't paid up, and I haven't pushed it because I wanted some time with her first—but I bet you whatever my salary is there's something there that can help us."

Sam knew what Roger's question was going to be. She hated that he'd decided to prioritize the topic, but she supposed the answer would put at least a few nagging annoyances to rest. She suspected Driff knew what her father was about to say, too, but the elf seemed content to let him go through the motions—or perhaps to make him work for it.

"Driff, where the hell are my wife's memories?"

LAZARUS

A DEVIANT MAGIC SHORT STORY

I 've got it!" Lazzy said, triumphantly presenting Keighlan with the unicorn's tooth.

She brushed a strand of hair out of her face and leaned in for a closer look. "Where was it?"

"In his desk drawer, underneath a pile of pens," Lazzy said proudly. "I knew Professor Lindzen would have one!"

"That's the last ingredient for the counter-spell," Keighlan replied, her smile beaming right into Lazzy's heart. "Now we just have to mix it all together, and then we can save Dash and Gearix!"

An ominous knock on the door ruined their celebration. "Professor?" a familiar gravelly voice asked. "You all right in there? You're not normally up this late."

It was Ranster, the groundskeeper. Lazzy would recognize that growl anywhere—and if Ranster caught them trespassing in a professor's office after curfew, there'd be hell to pay. They might even get expelled.

Ranster's keyring jangled as he searched for the one that would open the door.

His heart in his throat, Lazzy's eyes desperately searched the small room for a solution. That door was the only way in or out. Bookshelves packed time with tomes and papers stretched from the floor to the ceiling, covering the walls. A little sitting area with a pair of chairs and a small table offered no help.

The desk.

Keighlan's sharp mind was already there. She grabbed Lazzy's wrist and led him around the massive desk. The space underneath would just barely accommodate a pair of teenagers. He waved Keighlan under first. If it came to it, he could hand her the tooth, give himself up, and tell Ranster *he was alone. At least then she wouldn't be expelled, and she'd have a chance to save their friends.*

It was, indeed, a tight fit. Even though Keighlan had scrunched herself in as deeply as she could, Lazzy still barely managed to get himself into that space. They sat facing each other, legs pulled up tight against their chests. Lazzy was acutely aware of the warmth of her body and the way her left knee pressed against his right. Butterflies performed complex aerial maneuvers in his stomach as his fingers grazed the soft fabric of her skirt. Their gazes locked, and Lazzy lost himself in her beautiful green eyes.

The door opened—

"Hey, Amila!" Rondy gasped as he burst through the bushes and into her favorite reading nook behind the high school. He stumbled over his own feet, crashing to the grass at her side and knocking the paperback she'd been reading from her grasp.

Amila shoved the boy's hand out of her lap. "They're after you again, aren't they?"

Blushing, Rondy rolled onto his back and sighed. "Yeah. Chad hates it when I beat him at *Fortnite*."

She picked up her book and shook dirt out of it. "You are very lucky I didn't lose my place."

"*Lazarus Jones and the Curse of Obedience*," he read from the book's cover. "Really, Am? That's kid stuff."

She fixed him with her most pointed sixteen-year-old stare. "And your videogames aren't?"

"I'm going pro someday. You'll see." He sat up, smiling that cocksure smile that had convinced her to bail him out of so many dumb problems of his own making. "I'll make sure you have a prominent role in my entourage."

She slapped his arm with the book. "I am no one's *entourage*."

Rondy flinched away from the blow, feigning pain. "Did I say entourage? I meant bodyguard. Clearly your talents would be wasted elsewhere."

That wasn't quite what she wanted either, but she knew that was the best complement she was going to get out of him. "How many is it this time?"

"Chad, Todd 1, Todd 2, and all three of the McLeary kids," he replied. He slipped the onyx ring off his finger, killing the magic that kept his pointy ears cloaked. "Chad says he's going to break both of my thumbs and shove my controller up my ass."

She stifled a giggle. "Think it'll fit?"

"Hey! This is my future livelihood we're talking about here!"

"Then we have two choices," she said mischievously. "I can give you my own talisman so you can slip past them—again—or we can electrocute them."

"The second option," he replied quickly. "I like that one."

Amila had been hoping he'd say that. She'd wanted to show him what she could do all week. Knitting her brow in concentration, she pressed her thumb and forefinger together and then slowly drew them apart. A little bolt of lightning danced in the space between her digits.

Rondy gasped and flinched away. "Whoa! I was just joking! I didn't think you actually knew how to do it!"

"I've been practicing," she admitted. Speaking broke her concentration and killed the spell.

"I thought your mother hates magic."

She didn't like his accusatory tone. "I'm sixteen, Rondy. I can make my own decisions about this kind of thing." *And I'll be damned if I'm going to get caught defenseless ever again*, she added to herself.

"Well," he said with a frown, "just be careful. Especially around the humans."

"Can you imagine?" she asked happily, all the possibilities popping into and out of her mind. "One burst in Mrs. Emerson's science class and they'll have to throw out the whole damn book."

"Your mother won't like it if Evitankari comes sniffing around," he said. "My parents wouldn't like it either."

We could be so lucky, she thought. Her happiest dreams all involved elven agents descending on their Chicago suburb, identifying the obvious talent in Amila and Rondy, and bringing them back to the capital.

No more dumb humans. No more obnoxious hiding. No more pretending to be something she wasn't.

"I'll be careful," she replied. "I assume you want to borrow it, as usual."

He pressed his palms together in a desperate gesture. "Pleeeeeeeeease."

She made a show of thinking about it, even though her answer was never in doubt. "Fine. But you owe me one."

"Thanks, Am! I owe you like twenty."

"I know." But really, she'd brought it upon herself. The first time had been her idea. Any small inconvenience was worth it to help her only elven friend.

She looked away as she unclasped her pendant and pulled it away from her neck. Her ears and face vibrated as the magic cloaking them dissipated. Before she turned back to Rondy, she brushed a few locks of her hair down over the scarring on her cheek. He'd seen it before, but that didn't stop her from being self-conscious about it.

Sometimes she daydreamed about telling him where it came from. What would he think if he knew her father had wounded her with his magic as she and her mother had fled their former home in Germany? Would he encourage her to explore her magic if he knew her father was still out there? Would he do the dumb boy thing and get overprotective? Would he abandon her entirely? She didn't know, and that lack of confidence stilled her tongue as it always had.

He took and the pendant and handed her his ring. Even on her thumb it felt a little loose, but it would do. The air around the tips of her ears went fizzy as the magic hid her most prominent elven characteristic from the world.

The pendant Amila used was significantly more powerful than his ring. Her mother had splurged on a talisman that projected an unscarred version of her face as a means of covering up her scars. One moment, Rondy was a handsome teenage boy with a bright smile and piercing blue eyes. The next, Amila found herself looking into the mirror. She gasped. Seeing her own face plastered over Rondy's, above his thick neck and underneath his short, sandy hair, was always a shock.

He tossed her a pack of gum he pulled from his pocket. "Thank you so much, Am! You're a lifesaver!"

And then he burst back through the bushes, safe once more from those who would do him harm. Amila shook her head and returned to her book.

Keighlan pressed her hand to her mouth and whispered into it. Her fingers tightened around the words and her eyes flashed as she imbued them with power. Then she flicked her fist toward the hallway, releasing the enchanted whisper as if she were tossing something over her shoulder.

"Ranster, come quick!" a girl's voice echoed from the hallway. "Lazzy's in the begonias again!"

"Damn that kid!" the groundskeeper growled. His footfalls pounded the floor as he left the door and hurried down the corridor.

Lazzy raised an eyebrow at Keighlan, who stifled a giggle. "I'm in the begonias again? Really?"

She shrugged. "I couldn't think of anything that would make Ranster angrier."

Amila paused before turning the page. "Come on, Lazzy," she said to the paperback. "Kiss the clever magic girl who keeps saving your butt."

—⊂●⊃—

READ ON FOR A SNEAK PEAK OF THE FIRST TWO CHAPTERS OF *VENGEANCE SQUAD,* BOOK 5 OF THE DEVIANT MAGIC SERIES.

—⊂●⊃—

— CHAPTER ONE —

Ren Roberts couldn't tear his eyes away from the television screen. He and his mother had watched the grainy cell phone video of Tallisker's Detroit headquarters exploding five, six, maybe seven times. *The curse of 24-hour network news,* he thought morbidly. The outcome never changed, no matter how hard he willed it. One moment that stretch of midwestern skyline stood empty and blue, the next one of Tallisker's infamous hidden towers exploded in a tremendous fireball that turned the surrounding block into a crater and sent debris raining down upon the city.

Ren wondered if his father had become a single piece of that debris or if he'd been blasted into several. The latter seemed more likely, but he supposed it didn't matter. Any recognizable parts would be scooped up and disposed of by Tallisker's fixers. Ed Roberts had always joked that there'd be nothing in his casket.

Ellen Roberts sat on the coffee table in front of Ren, beside his untouched afternoon scotch. She held her phone so tightly to her ear that Ren worried it might become permanently attached.

"Pick up, Eddie," she muttered every time she dialed. "Please pick up."

On screen, the billowing pillar of smoke was replaced with a shot of 24 Hour Cable News Barbie sitting behind a curved desk in a slick studio trimmed with important looking computer generated bullshit. "Just who is this Tallisker Corporation?" she asked with perfect vaguely southern diction, her dark eyes wide with concern. "How does a multinational operation hide a skyscraper in plain sight?"

Well, you see, Ren's mental voice said with a heavy dose of parental knowhow, *when elves and demons decide they hate humanity very, very much, they put their heads together and use their magic to conceal all the important shit.*

"Why hasn't this story been squelched?" he mused to his highball, because he knew his mother wasn't listening. "Tallisker has armies of publicists, lawyers, and thugs who's only job is keeping the company's name out of the news."

Ellen pried her phone from her ear, punched a button on the touchscreen, and then reattached the device to her skull. "Pick up, Ed. Please."

Ren's mother had been on her way to book club when the news hit. She was still dressed like a Patagonia model: designer jeans, brown puffer vest over a flannel shirt, her blonde hair up in a ponytail, just enough makeup to look good in a selfie with some friendly wildlife. Though he hadn't seen her face since they'd sat down, he knew her lip would be curled and her eyes bloodshot. The fingers of her free hand flicked back and forth across her wedding ring.

The wild corporate swinger parties just won't be the same, Ren thought evilly. A pang of something shot through his gut. Guilt? No, that couldn't have been in it. Hunger, he decided. Or maybe just gas.

"Tallisker's complex web of holdings is nearly impossible to decipher," a middle-aged hipster in an offputting courdoroy jacket explained, live on location from what appeared to be his dining room. In the panel beside him, the anchor pursed her lips and shook her head. "Are they a finical services corporation? A secretive defense contractor? An experimental biomedical laboratory? Dangerous arms dealers? My research suggests they're all of the above, and more. The truth's somewhere down a dark rabbit hole I can't find the bottom of."

"Eddie," Ellen pleaded, trying to spin her ring right through her finger. "Come on."

Ren knew how this particular story ended. His father had been drilling it into his head for as long as he could remember. The families of Tallisker executives allowed the demonic bastards to desperately clutch to a few shreds of their waning humanity, providing a safe harbor in the storm of madness threatening to break their grips on reality. Ed, true to form, had genuinely loved his wife and son—but that love had made Ren and Ellen significant targets even in the best of times. Removing or converting a rival's family was a great way to climb the corporate ladder or secure your position. A particularly vile piece of work named Demson had made it no secret that he wanted to make Ren his protege, likely as a means of slowing or halting Ed's rise toward the board, or ensuring that he'd play along once he got there. Ren didn't want to turn into a beastly personification of evil. He'd always been content as a lay follower of the world's lesser vices. And so he'd stayed in Harksburg, within his father's protective sphere, despite the opportunities offered by his family's wealth.

"Edwarrrrrrrrrrrrrd. Please."

The primary anchor appeared relieved to be alone on screen again. "Authorities are evacuating an area two square miles around the fallen skyscraper, lending credence to social media reports of chemical spills and clouds of strage gasses."

Ed Roberts's territory offered no security without the threat of the man himself enforcing it. That meant it was time for Ren to leave.

But where could he go? Life on the run or in hiding wouldn't inherently be any safer than staying put. A deceased Tallisker executive's family still held value as a grotesque display of power and influence, or even just as a means of satisfying an overactive ego. Demson or one of Ed's other rivals would find him eventually. Ren couldn't stand the thought of spending every waking hour looking over his shoulder for the pursuers he knew were just a step behind him.

"Pick up, pick up, pick up."

An interesting idea pushed pierced the dark clouds hanging ominously in Ren's mind like a beam of morning sunshine. He considered it for a moment, and then took a hit of his forgotten scotch and considered it a moment more to make sure the idea held up. "This was an inside job, wasn't it?"

His mother nodded. "Guaranteed. No one's dumb enough to take that kind of shot at Tallisker except Tallisker itself."

"My thoughts exactly," he replied with a tip of his glass and a triumph swig.

It wasn't much to go on, but it was better than waiting around for the inevitable, and Ren possessed something he doubted the board's own investigators had: a sneaking suspicion that recent events in Harksburg, of which he'd been a key part, were somehow related to his father's summons to Detroit and that building's subsequent destruction.

Ren finished his drink. "I'm going out for a bit," he declared, rising slowly against a stiff pair of knees. "I need to have a chat with Death."

— CHAPTER TWO —

"Eric Pepper," Ren said as he wrote the same with his brand new mechanical pencil in a freshly procured Moleskine. "Assistant Manager for International Waste Relations. Dad reported multiple awkward interactions with this individual in the eleventh floor bathroom to HR."

Ren surveyed the ring of dirt around his perch, wracking his memory. He'd already filled seven pages with the name and misdeeds of Tallisker employees who'd interfaced even remotely negatively with Ed Roberts. Demson, of course, got the first page all to himself. Few of the others possessed the kind of stroke required to summon his father to Detroit—as far as Ren knew, at least—but he thought it wise to cast a wide net. Perhaps a few of them had worked together, or maybe one of the lesser middle managers who had nothing to do with Ed's death would recognize his vulnerable family as an opportunity.

He'd taken up residence in the driver's seat of the broken down bulldozer watching over the usual gathering place in the Works, the site of a long abandoned attempt to stimulate Harksburg's economy with an injection of industry. In a way, he supposed, the amount of money spent on partying out there on the outskirts of town sort of justified the aborted effort. The night was cool, crisp, and clear, though Ren worried the light breeze would become a frosty slap in the face as the evening progressed. He'd left the firepit unlit, ostensibly so he could focus on buffing up his Tallisker notes but really because he'd never once been able to light the damn thing. Such tasks, he'd long ago decided, were best left to his blue collar companions.

A stroke of inspiration set his pen into motion. "Brian Drew," he said as he wrote, "reassigned to the Edmonton office because Ed hated his whistling."

Ren studied this one for a few moments, as he had several others, his pen wriggling in anticipation of angrily scratching out such a stupid incident. He turned the page, keeping it—for now. "This'd be a lot fucking easier if these fucking demons weren't such a bunch of petty fucking children," he said to the glass of scotch sitting beside him. That went for both his father and his numerous potential rivals.

He leaned back into the ratty couch cushions some enterprising drunk had recently duct taped to the broken down bulldozer's rusty seat, picturing Ed Roberts at the dinner table as vividly as if he were once again a seven year old in his family's dining room instead of alone out in the Works. The man leaned his elbows heavily on the table cloth, his scraggly chest hair puffing out from his unbuttoned dress shirt as if straining for a bite of roast beef. Cheap whiskey sloshed out of his highball and all over his fingers as he worked himself into a furor. "That motherfucker," his father snarled. Ellen shoveled a forkful of potatoes into her mouth without blinking, long ago having given up on maintaining any sort of propriety at the dinner table when her husband came home all worked up. "That motherfucker Eric Pepper," Ed said again as little Ren watched on in awe, "had the *gall* to sneak up *right* behind me while I was *pissing* in the *urinal* and grabbed my hips and say *errrrr hey there Eddie errrrr need a hand with that*? And then he laughed. He *laughed*." Ed brought his hand down on the table hard enough to make the silverware dance a little jig.

Ren flipped back a page and circled Eric Pepper's name in his notebook. No way that guy got off with just a stern talking to from HR. Ed would've lit his car on fire or at least ruined his credit score, or maybe tried to toss him out a window when no one was looking. That one would be carrying a grudge for sure.

His appointment emerged from the woods along the usual path just on time. Ren had always been able to set his watch to Kevin Felton. The man's awkward smile was right there in the dictionary beside words like "punctual," "conscientious," "scrupulous," and, frankly, "fussy," which was one of the main reasons they'd been best friends since the day they first met in kindergarten. Their individual neuroses meshed perfectly.

A tinge of disappointment shivered up Ren's spine when he noticed Nella at Kevin's side. He still wasn't quite sure to make of his best friend's new girlfriend. She seemed nice enough, and she was certainly way too hot for a dork like Kevin Felton, but she'd also strung him along for years before only recently revealing that she was, in fact, a real person who'd been sneaking into his bedroom for midnight booty calls and not just some recurring wet dream with a strange blue skintone. Ren couldn't fathom forgiving that kind of thing as quickly as Kevin had.

Then again, none of Ren's exes had dumped him to pursue a career as a professional fuck toy for a bunch of Tallisker middle managers, so he supposed some leeway had to be granted.

"I brought the good stuff," Kevin said, raising a bottle of twenty year old Glenlivet. He'd worn his favorite outfit—a black leather jacket and a pair of black jeans—and the wind had already mussed his unruly brown hair.

"We're gonna need it," Ren replied. He stashed the notebook in his peacoat's interior pocket and swung himself down from the bulldozer.

"Got some cheap swill too," Nella added with a glance down toward the dual six packs she carried, "to distract the riff-raff." Her clothes matched her boyfriend's, though she'd worn higher heels and not a single strand of her long black hair had fallen out of place.

Ren bristled inwardly at the way she'd inserted herself into the group. Who the hell did she think she was, and why the fuck did she think she could ply Kevin's friends with cheap mass market booze? Her strategy was sound, of course, but she hadn't been employing it for a decade-plus like Ren and Kevin and so her use of it was presumptuous at best. Ren deployed his brightest smile anyway. "As clever as she is beautiful. Remind me again why you're walking around with this troglodyte on your arm?"

"He doesn't litter and his mother's nice," Nella replied without hesitation. Ren remained impassive but mentally assigned her a few positive points on his scorecard.

The new arrivals stopped their approach a few feet away, right beside the old dozer's blade. Ren and Kevin stared at each other for a few moments. Things were about to change and they both knew it. Ren flashed back to that day—fuck, almost ten years ago—when he'd wished Kevin the best of luck as he and Mrs. Felton packed up the car to move him off to college in the big city. He'd hated how stupidly emotional his best friend's departure had made him. Those same butterflies fluttered around Ren's chest again, lighting up every nerve they touched and setting him on fire. He still hated the sensation.

"I'm sorry about your father," Kevin finally said.

Ren's butterflies sprouted knives on the tips of their wings. "Ah," he grunted, buying time to find the words, "thanks. We always figured a grisly end for Ed Roberts was only a matter of time. The man's taste in business associates was pretty terrible." A bright smile stretched his face. "Dad should've quit the moment he found out they hired your ex."

Nella's eyebrows leapt up toward her scalp. Despite her obvious efforts, she hadn't fully acclimated to the god-tier level of bullshitting their friend group lived and breathed. The really bad stuff still caught her off guard. Ren decided that was kind of cute.

Kevin, however, grinned like a madman. "No shit!" he replied merrily. "That one ruins everything she touches."

Ren flicked his eyes down to his friend's crotch. "Shame."

"That part made it through just fine," Nella interjected smoothly, "although he still cries himself to sleep a few times a week." Ren toasted her with a nod and a tip of his glass.

Kevin grunted just as he had everyday in fourth grade when someone disparaged his off-brand Chicago Bears jacket. "We should probably get the complicated parts of this out of the way before the rest of the party gets here."

It was Ren's turn to grunt once again. "I hadn't intended for this to turn into yet another high school reunion."

"I figured someone needed to plan your going away party. That's what you're about to tell me, right? That you're going on the run so Tallisker can't find you?"

That question burrowed into Ren's gut like a barely sharpened stick. In anticipation of Kevin's lack of insight into Tallisker's horrifying corporate culture, Ren had prepared a long-winded, thoroughly well-sourced explanation of why his father's death necessited his flight from the only home he'd ever known. He had everything but Powerpoint slides and handouts, the latter only because his useless printer had run out of toner again. "How the hell did you know that?" he asked.

"My new job," Kevin replied, the guilt thick on his tongue. "Maeve Remini over in Bilton explained it all to me." When Kevin didn't elaborate further, Nella elbowed him in the kidney. "She'd been burned alive," he sputtered.

Ren emptied his glass with a long swig and set it down on the bulldozer's tread. Then he snatched the fresh bottle from his friend's hand and began working at the wrapper with his thumbnail. He'd met Maeve a couple years ago at the local Tallisker branch's family picnic. Nice person, albeit a bit naive about the company and her wife's role in it, and the beaded belts she made as a hobby sucked. "Anyone else?"

"Clint Pope in Hanton," Kevin said sadly. "Same cause of death. Whoever it was took the kids."

The map in Ren's head suddenly turned ominous. "They're headed this way."

"Sorry!" Kevin snapped as his body suddenly went rigid. "Gotta get to work."

And then he was gone. The little part of the Works Kevin Felton had filled mere moments ago now stood empty. Neither Ren nor Nella so much as blinked at his disappearance. They'd seen it before. The prospect of being left alone together, however, was jarring.

The water nymph recovered first. "Guess it's time for a beer," she said, setting the six packs down on the ground and withdrawing a single bottle.

"And a scotch," Ren added, finally opening the expensive Glenlivet. He poured a couple fingers into his glass and studied the brown liquor as he swirled it around. A quick drink warmed his throat and settled his nerves. "You look better in blue."

She smiled. "Oh, I agree, but Kev worries what the neighbors might think." As Ren flinched at the disgusting nickname she'd bestowed upon his best friend, Nella reached back over her collarbone and released the clasp on her necklace. Her pale caucasian skin turned a a healthy shade of light blue as the necklace's enchantment dissipated. "For you, because you're leaving, but Rot, I fucking swear I will ruin every bottle of alcohol you own if Oscar or Doorknob or any of the others catch me like this." She punctuated her threat with an annoyed flutter of the gills in either side of her neck.

Another awkward silence settled upon them like the eveing's mist rolling into a port town. "Take care of Felton for me," Ren blurted. His cheeks flushed. "Wanted to get that out while we had some privacy."

Nella nodded. "I will." The sharp *crack-hiss* as she twisted the cap on her beer seemed to second her. "Is Ellen leaving with you?"

Ren took another drink. "She's going to the follow Dad's plan. He left us a list of safehouses and people he trusted." The statement reminded him of how his parents' swinger lifestyle had partly been a means of building out the family's options in the result of the unthinkable, and then he finished his glass.

"Obviously you don't think that's a good idea."

"Of course not. It'd be naive to think one of these demon bastards hasn't put a similar level of preparation into hunting Ed Roberts's wife and son as he put into trying to protect them. Us."

"And she doesn't like whatever you're planning?"

"No," he said, his hands shaking as he poured himself a fresh beverage. "She laughed at me. Said I've got a death wish." *Like my father.*

Nella took a sip of her beer and then held the bottle out in front of her, underneath her free palm."It would be my pleasure to offer her another option."

As Ren watched, droplets of water rose up out of the bottle's mouth to collect in a growing sphere beneath the nymph's hand. The flow stopped a few seconds later when the sphere reached the size of a golf ball. It jiggled and then flattened into a shape like a hockey puck. Nella's eyes widened as she took a deep breath. When she exhaled, the moisture she collected flashed like a little strobe. She quickly flipped her hand around to catch the falling wafer of bright blue crystal she'd created.

"This grants the bearer entry to Talvayne and an audience with the king," she said, holding the token out to Ren.

He plucked it from her palm and held it up where he could get a better look at it. The trio of fish shaped runes carved into its face, their tails touching in the center and their open mouths facing outward toward the edges, was unmistakable. "I didn't know you're royalty," Ren said with a deep bow. "M'lady."

Nella's cheeks flushed purple. "My family's a distant offshoot of the current king's line. We're not on the best of terms, but that token cannot be refused."

Ren pocketed the little tablet. "Your wisdom, like your beauty, knows no bounds, m'lady. Thank you."

She shook the beer bottle and grinned evilly. "Stop that right now, or by royal decree I will force you to drink the vile, partially dehydrated sludge remaining in this vessel."

"Anything but that, please." He raised a single finger to indicate the arrival of a brilliant idea. "Let's give it to Spuddner. Peel the label off and we'll tell him it's a hot new craft beer from the city."

"Don't tell Kev," *cringe*, "but I like the way you think." She set to work on the corner of the label with her fingernail.

"You're not going to at least *try* to talk me into going to Talvayne?"

"Would it work?"

"No."

"Then I'm going to take my boyfriend's advice and not waste my time." The flimsy label tore off in a single piece with a satisfying *slurp*. Nella flicked it onto the ground like a snot.

Kevin Felton popped back into existence beside them. He'd obviously taken a moment to fix his hair before returning. "Heart attack in Green River. Nothing to worry about. What'd I miss?"

"I gave him the thing for his mother and we agreed on a plan to mess with Oscar," Nella replied.

"Don't explain about that second part," Kevin said gleefully. "I want to be surprised."

"I've got one more piece of business before I allow you to drink your faces off in my honor," Ren said, fighting the the beginning of a slur. "Felton, what happened in the middle of everything last week that I don't know about?"

The reaper's eyes narrowed. "You don't honestly think I'm hiding something, do you?"

"Absolutely not. I've always admired and respected your candor. I wonder, however, if perhaps you experienced or heard anything you initially dismissed as unimportant or coincidental, or maybe that you didn't understand at the time. You are relatively new to all this secretive magic shit, after all."

"You're looking for a connection between your father's death and what went down with Billy," Nella said insightfully. Kevin's eyes widened, the gears in his mind obviously struggling to get up to speed.

"Bingo," Ren replied. "Driff stuck his nose in Billy's business at Tallisker's request. I'm thinking it may not be a coincidence that someone scheduled Harksburg's preeminent business demon for a week of meetings in a soon to be eradicated office not long after the conclusion of the elf's intervention."

He looked to Kevin. "Who's Rotreego? Driff almost shat himself when you said that name."

Kevin blanched and plucked the bottle of dehydrated beer from his girlfriend's grasp. Nella pursed her lips but didn't protest. "Another elf," he said. "We were prisoners together, in my neighbor's basement. He said he was the Pantari."

Ren groaned. "The Pintiri? Ffffffffffffffffffffuck."

"You only elongate your f-bombs when something's really bad," Kevin said, considering the bottle in his hand.

"The Pintiri's their ringer, or maybe their enforcer," Nella explained. "He or she wields what's often considered the world's most powerful direct offensive magic. That magic resides in and flows through the Pintiri's weapon."

Kevin nodded dumbly, as if she'd just spoken a completely different language. "Rotreego said his magic sword didn't work anymore, and that my neighbor killed him several times. With Billy off the job...it didn't stick."

A pair of distant neurons flared to life and linked up in Ren's brain. "Nella, the Pintiri's magic is released from his weapon upon his death, right? Then the next in line has to go get it?"

"Supposedly," she said softly, her eyes wide, "but what happens if the last Pintiri doesn't stay dead?"

That question hung over the trio for several moments. Kevin frowned and scratched the back of his head, clearly struggling to work it all out. Ren's train of thought barreled down the same old track it had traveled countless times: toward the money. Somehow, some way, someone had set this Rotreego character up for his or her own benefit. Who stood to profit from the world's first living former Pintiri? The answer proved elusive, and yet Ren felt certain it tied into the attack on Tallisker's Detroit headquarters.

Kevin sighed and took a drink. Ren and Nella watched expectantly as he slowly raised the tainted bottle to his lips. The vile liquor exploded back out of his mouth as soon as it touched his tongue, spattering Ren right in the face.

"I assume that was intended for Oscar," Kevin sputtered, coughing as he wiped his face.

Ren pulled a handkerchief out of his coat's interior pocket and rubbed down his own mug, fighting the urge to retch. The overpowering malt smell of that sticky dehydrated beer set his head spinning.

"There's a witch, too," Kevin blurted out. "A *fucking* witch, in Driff's words. I don't think they get along."

Ren tossed the wet handkerchief under the bulldozer's blade in disgust. "Never heard of any witches, but I'll keep that information in mind. Any idea where Rotreego is now?"

"The dude was so embarrassed that he threatened to geld me if I told anyone he needed my help with Mr. Gregson. He's probably long gone. "

"Actually," Nella interjected, "he's hiding out at Donovan's. He went straight there after he escaped your neighbor."

Kevin frowned. "How'd you know that?"

"My book club meets there every Wednesday at lunchtime. He drunkenly tried to convince Barbara that JFK was killed by a werewolf who owed a major gambling debt to Hoover. Strange guy."

"That doesn't sound like the Rotreego I know. He didn't say anything obnoxiously self-centered or that indicates a deep case of depression?"

She shook her head. "No, he just seemed a little...off, and sort of cheerful in a way, too."

Ren spotted movement in the forest on the other side of the clearing. The local talent was on its way. "I'll go to Donovan's tomorrow," he said. Although time was certainly of the essence, he figured it would be easier to deal with Rotreego when the fairy bar would be less busy—and he never would've admitted it, but he wanted nothing more than to get totally fucking shithoused with all of his oldest friends one last time.

"Hey there assholes!" Oscar Spuddner squealed as he and Doorknob lurched out of the forest, each struggling with the weight of a cheap thirty rack and their broad, toothy smiles. "Party's not over yet, is it?"

With a gasp, Nella put her necklace back on, fumbling briefly with the clasp before it caught. Her blue skin turned a light shade of caucasian once again.

"Gentlemen!" Kevin declared, spreading his arms magnanimously as he turned to face Oscar and Doorknob—and strategically positioning himself to block his view of his magical girlfriend in case she needed a moment to conceal the parts of herself they might find confusing. "I wholeheartedly assure you that we have *not...yet...begun...to drink!*"

"Could you possibly be more gauche?" Ren spat.

"Seems highly likely," Kevin replied. Nella giggled.

The two new arrivals set their precious beverages down gingerly in front of the bulldozer. "Kevin told us about your operation," Doorknob said sheepishly. "I'm sorry you have to go through that."

Ren noticed his best friend's smirk out of the corner of his eye and decided to play along. "I appreciate that, my good sir."

Oscar wiped a tendril of sweat from his brow with the brim of his old Cubs hat. "He told us everything. Me, I had no idea you had to go all the way to Boston to get your prosthetic testicles replaced every ten years!"

Kevin snorted. Nella elbowed him in the side.

As far as cover stories went, Ren supposed it would do—and that it was wholly appropriate, given the source. He refilled his highball and raised it to his friends as his devious mind, warped further by alcohol, fear, and something like grief for a father he couldn't really describe his feelings toward, generated what it considered to be the perfect toast for the entirety of his situation. "Well then: here's to good friends, and to my new pair of balls!"

— ACKNOWLEDGEMENTS —

Thank you, as always, for reading my work. Playing in this crazy world I've built is so much more fun knowing there people out there who enjoy it. I am super fortunate to be able to take a silly little idea like "there's no way all these young adult fiction heroes all grow up to be perfectly adjusted adults."

I'd like to thank Gwendolyn Nix for her editorial contributions and Anne Marie Cochran for the amazing cover art.

And as always, I'd like to give a major shout out to Jeremy Mohler, Alana Joli Abbott, and the rest of the team at Outland Entertainment for helping me bring this work to the masses.

For more by Scott Colby, check out www.deviantmagic.com.

— ABOUT THE AUTHOR —

Frustrated with the generic, paint-by-numbers state of modern fantasy writing, Scott Colby is working hard to give the genre the kick in the pants it so desperately needs. Shouldn't stories about people and creatures with the power to magically change the world around them be creative, funny, and kind of weird? Scott thinks so.

Check out deviantmagic.com for more from Scott Colby.